DANCING ON AIR

NANCY LOYAN

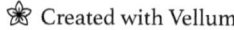 Created with Vellum

Performers of Middle Eastern Dance

1

Waiting in the café's lobby was like watching the loading of Noah's Ark. Being single in a two-by-two world could be unsettling. So much for Friday night "date night." Out of the corner of her eye, Meg observed a man leaning against a pillar, his gaze glued on his smart phone. His profile was classically handsome. Tall, his lean body was encased in distressed jeans and a buffalo plaid shirt, tucked in at his slim waist. He looked like a catalog model. He was probably waiting for his date to appear. Men who looked like him wouldn't be alone. They never were.

A couple rose from a far table, ready to leave the crowded café.

The hostess appeared in the lobby, holding two menus. "Table for two?"

The guy looked up, and shrugged.

Meg shrugged as well. "Table for one?"

The hostess shook her head. "Only a table for two."

"I don't know about you, but I'm hungry, and tired of waiting. We can share a table, if you don't mind," the man said, shoving his phone in his pants' pocket, and meeting her startled gaze.

His emerald eyes were soft. She was able to see every plane and angle on his face, framed by shaggy, sandy-colored hair. Sharing a table in a popular restaurant, with a handsome man wasn't such a bad idea.

"Sure, why not?" Meg answered.

"Great."

They followed the hostess to the table in a back corner. The man sat against the wall, and she across from him.

"We actually lucked out," he said, picking up a menu. "It's a popular little place. The food packs them in."

"That's why it's a personal favorite," she said, reaching for a menu.

He handed it to her. "Come here often?"

"I plan on it. I've been here only twice before. I'm rather new in town," she admitted.

"You live here, in Cairo?" he asked, his gaze hypnotic.

She drew a deep breath. "I do. Do you?"

"Outside of town, a few freeway exits beyond."

"I see."

"Cairo is a quaint little town, a mix of suburbia and rural life. It's a friendly place, and it has the cute, wholesome factor. Heck, this place is called, The Coffee Cup Bistro. How fitting." He chuckled.

His laugh was deep and fun. She had to smile.

What was she doing, she asked herself? Meeting a charming man was not on her agenda. She had come to Cairo to literally run away from her life in L.A. She had looked at a road atlas, decided on a small town in the Midwest, and her finger pointed to Cairo, a strange name for a town that seemed to be in the middle of nowhere. She had been born in the middle of nowhere, and decided that she needed to go back to find herself. A man was not part of her plans.

She picked up the menu, and perused the selections, though she had already made up her mind from the insert of specials. The man across from her seemed to be analyzing his menu. She took a moment to observe him. Handsome men were a dime a dozen where she came from, and they all pursued her for the wrong reasons. Being with a man who treated her as a normal woman was refreshing, in an unusual way. She had forgotten how it felt to be normal.

The waitress came by for their orders.

"Ladies first." The man put down his menu, and deferred to her.

"I'll have the Buffalo chicken wrap with fresh cut fries, and coleslaw," she ordered, handing the waitress her menu.

"Sir?"

"The roast beef sandwich au jus, with sweet potato fries, and coleslaw. A Guinness on tap, too." The waitress took his menu.

The waitress smiled. "Together, or separate?"

"Separate," Meg said.

"Put her wine on my tab," the man added.

"I didn't order any wine," Meg said, confused.

He winked. "I think you should. Chardonnay?"

How did he know that it was her preferred drink?

"Why not? Chardonnay it is."

When the waitress left, she stared at him. "Why are you buying me a drink?"

"It's Friday night. Everyone needs a drink on Friday. Did you think that I was going to get you drunk, and ravish you?" He chuckled.

Maybe that wasn't a bad idea, she thought, since she hadn't been ravished in years ... or ever. She cleared her throat, and the thought.

"So, what do you do for a living, Misses? Miss? Ms.?"

She hesitated. Of course, she couldn't tell him the truth. It would ruin the spontaneity, the fun, and her anonymity.

He was awaiting an answer.

"I, I'm a waitress in a diner." She remembered seeing a retro diner a town away.

"The Belle Diner?"

She nodded. Great, he knew the place, and she was an awful liar, though actresses were supposed to be good at it.

"And you're going out to eat on a Friday night?"

"Um, why not? I like to be served once in a while."

"I get it." He sat back in his chair.

"So, what do you do for a living?"

He raked his hair with his hand. "Just a tow motor operator."

"I see." A blue-collar guy. She hadn't met one of those, since she was a struggling teenager.

"Honest wages, for an honest day's work," he said, staring at her, as if awaiting a reaction.

"Nothing wrong with that." There wasn't. Actually, she preferred to be with someone who had a normal job, and a normal life. She had grown tired of people who had more money than they could spend, yet were living lies, and suffering from unhappiness. She had been one of those people. It's why she landed in a placed called Cairo.

Their wine and beer arrived.

"A toast," he lifted his frothy mug.

"To what?"

"Let's see. To your arriving in Cairo. To sharing a table and conversation."

"That should do it." She lifted her glass of wine.

He tapped his mug to her glass, and they drank.

"You know, this sure beat eating alone," he said.

"I have to agree."

She had been eating bagged salads, and carry-out alone

since she arrived in town, usually in her small apartment. Not knowing anyone had its advantages, and disadvantages.

"I don't mean to pry, but where are you from, and what brought you to Cairo?" he asked, leaning forward.

She hadn't made up a viable story, and feared that her lies would catch up to her one day. It was bad enough that she said that she worked at a diner, where she hadn't even eaten. As an actress, whose life revolved around pretending, why was making up stories about herself so difficult?

"I left a bad relationship, and came here to start over," she explained, hoping that he wouldn't pry.

"I see. Life happens." He sighed.

Their food arrived, and the focus was on eating.

He had impeccable manners, she thought, for a tow motor operator.

"Here we are having dinner together, and I don't even know your name?" he asked.

"Meg Miller. Just call me Meg. And, you?"

"River Rutledge. Just call me River."

The name suited him.

"With a name like that, you should be in Hollywood," she said.

"Sorry, I'm afraid that I'm not leading man material." He scoffed.

She had to disagree. With his rugged good looks, manner, and name, he would probably do well. After all, she should know.

After dinner, they paid their respective checks, and he escorted her outside.

"I'll walk you to your car," he offered.

"I walked. I live just up the street."

He seemed a little disappointed. "I see."

She walked with him to where a "beater" Chevy was

parked. The car had more dents than a moon crater, and needed a paint job, badly.

"My ride," he said. "It runs."

"Hey, that's all that matters."

He put out his hand, and she shook it. A weird electrical current passed between them, that she couldn't explain.

"Great meeting you, Meg. Perhaps, we can meet again. Same place, for dinner?" he asked.

"That would be fun," she replied.

"How do I reach you?"

She pointed up the street. "I live in the apartment above The Classy Chassis fashion store."

2

Meg loved her apartment. Though the size of one of her rooms in her Hollywood mansion, it was intimate, warm, and it was hers. It didn't require a staff to maintain or pay, and no one knew her business. The best part was that it had come partially furnished. The previous tenant left the green sofa, the brocade chairs, and end table near the bay window, and the brass lamp. The rest of the space was empty. She had yet to furnish the bedroom, and didn't know what to do with the extra bedroom, with its cute African animal murals pasted on the walls. Her suitcases were open on the floor, as she had been living out of them. Such a simple existence was a throwback to the years when she was a young ingenue, starving actress. Maybe she needed to go back in time to discover where she was going.

Her mind wandered to the handsome stranger that she had dined with the previous evening. She told him that she was a waitress at the Belle Diner. Heck, she hadn't worked as a waitress since her teens. Maybe she needed to start over, by going back to where she had been. On a whim, she wondered if she still remembered the schtick. Heck, if the handsome guy appeared at the diner, looking for her, and she wasn't working there, what would he think? Did she want to live a total lie? She had to have a job to complete the disguise. This was crazy. If her agent, publicist, and fans knew that she was waitressing in a diner, would they be surprised? She shook her head, laughing.

So far, no one recognized her. Apparently, looking like her plain, ordinary self, drew little attention. Allowing her hair to grow out, she dyed it back to its original mousy brown. Without the foundation, blush, highlighter and contouring, liner and false lashes, manicured brows, and bright lipstick, she was scrubbed-fresh ordinary. Wearing baggy tunics hid her statuesque frame, and made her less Dolly Parton, and more matron. Going back to her old nickname also didn't raise any red flags. This was one acting role she could relate to. If she hadn't left home to pursue her dreams, this is what she probably would have looked like.

Working as a waitress was probably all she would have qualified for. After all, she didn't attend college. After high school, she packed her bags and headed to L.A. Her first job was as a waitress in a diner. To most people, the idea of going back to being a waitress would be preposterous. After all, she didn't need money, or a job. Maybe she just needed a purpose.

As crazy as it was, she had driven cross country from L.A. to Cairo. Catching a plane would have been impossible. The paparazzi would have been on her like buzzards over a carcass. Pretending she was hired help, after dying her hair, and removing her makeup, and dressing in cheap, drab clothes, she snuck out of her mansion. She bought a used, stoic gray Ford Focus, for cash, and embarked on her journey. To keep her staff from reporting her AWOL, she left them the message that she was going on a sabbatical, and would keep in touch. Right.

She drove the Ford on the freeway to the Belle Diner. As luck would have it, a "Help Wanted" sign was plastered in the window of the streamlined silver diner, that resembled an old railroad car. She entered, just as staff was cleaning up after a busy breakfast crowd. She surveyed the red Naugahyde seats in the booths and on the chrome barstools, the long counter, glass display cases, and the work stations, and kitchen beyond. The scent of grease brought back memories of her arrival in California, and her first job. Her palms began to sweat, and she trembled, just as she had when she had applied for that job.

"May I help you?" a gruff-sounding woman, around fifty asked. Wiping her hands in her apron, she entered from the kitchen, and met Meg across the counter.

"I ... I wanted to apply for the waitressing job," Meg stuttered.

"Any experience?"

"I worked as a waitress in a diner when I was younger, and I thought that I could do so again, now that I need a job."

The woman rolled her eyes. "Let me guess, you got dumped by some jerk guy, and left with nothing. You are starting over, and need a job?"

Meg smiled. The woman could have been a script writer. "Yes, as a matter of fact."

"Great."

Meg tilted her head.

"We've been short-handed around here, and could use some help. How much do you expect to get paid?"

Meg shrugged. She had been so far removed from the real world, she hadn't the foggiest idea.

"How about $7.50 an hour, plus tips? Part-time to start."

"Okay."

"Okay?"

Meg nodded.

"When can you start?"

"When do you want me to start?"

"I can start training you this afternoon, if you can make it."

"I can make it."

"Good. Come back at three. Wear black slacks and a white tee shirt, if you have them."

"It can be arranged."

MEG WONDERED why she was so giddy after she left the diner. You'd think that she won the leading role in a new Star War's film. This was a waitressing job, in a diner, for goodness sake. But it was a job that she landed on her own. No agent needed. No screen test.

After parking her car behind The Classy Chassis, she entered the clothing store, before going up to her apartment. Racks and circular rounders were filled with sportswear in a multitude of colors and sizes. The shop was a far cry from the fancy boutiques she had grown accustomed to, and farther yet from a prime seat at the New York City designer runway shows.

"May I help you?" a stylish woman, in her forties asked, and upon recognizing her as a tenant, said, "Meg."

Meg met the gaze of her landlady, Estelle. "Hi. I'm looking for some black slacks, and a white tee shirt. I'm starting a new job, and it's the required uniform."

"Serving, huh?"

Meg nodded. Estelle was probably surprised, since she paid three months' rent up front, in cash.

"Easy enough."

Estelle selected a few pairs of slacks and some tee shirts. "You can try these on."

Meg disappeared into the back-dressing room. She selected a pair of slacks. The tee shirts were a bit snug, and accented her figure a little too much. She didn't want to attract *that* kind of attention. She called out to Estelle, requesting some with a loose fit.

Estelle laughed. "You have an enviable figure. Why are you trying to hide it? You could get some really big tips."

If Estelle only knew. She left Hollywood to draw attention away from herself. "I don't want that kind of attention. Something loose-fitting please."

Estelle sighed. "Okay."

She returned with looser styles. "You know, you'd be a hit as a belly dancer."

Meg laughed. "I took private lessons. I'm not into performing."

"There's an amazing studio down the street. Kemsit's. She offers group and private lessons, if you're interested. I dance in her professional dance company, Pharaoh's Daughters."

"You dance?" Estelle seemed a bit prim and proper to be a belly dancer.

"Yes. Even I can transform into someone exotic." She winked.

"Down the street, you say?"

CALL HER CRAZY. The idea of taking private belly dance lessons sounded like fun. The exercise was something she would be needing, now that she was away from her personal trainer. After making her purchases, going up to her apartment for a quick salad lunch, she decided on a stroll down the street. Downtown Cairo exuded quaint. The Victorian era storefronts added charm. There was the grocery, pharmacy, hardware store, bank, The Coffee Cup Bistro, and Luke's Auto Garage. On the corner of North and Main, she saw an impressive mural of the Great Pyramids, and the sign for Kemsit Dance. The silhouette of a dancer in the glass, the purple and red curtains, fluttering, and Middle Eastern art objects on the window shelf belied its purpose. The etching on the door said, "Take a chance, dance." Why not?

She opened the glass door, and entered the sandlewood-incense- scented space. The wood floors were as shiny as the mirrors on the walls. The purple, fabric-draped ceiling, and floor pillows stacked in a corner, added a harem ambiance. Music befitting a snake charmer emanated from the speakers set in the corners of the ceiling. Impressive. This dance studio was nicer than many she had encountered in Hollywood.

"*Ahlan Wa Sahlan.* I'm Kemsit. Welcome to my *har'eem,*" an exotic vision in a black catsuit, and coin hip belt greeted. The stunning woman with wavy black hair and sapphire eyes could have easily outdone Elizabeth Taylor as Cleopatra.

"Hi. Estelle at The Classy Chassis recommended your studio. I thought that I'd inquire about private lessons."

"Have you danced before?"

"Actually, I have, when I lived in L.A. It was good exercise."

"Are you an actress?" Kemsit's gaze was piercing, as if she could see through her, and her disguise. She shifted on her feet.

"It didn't work out."

Kemsit smirked. "I see. What's your name?"

"Meg. Meg Miller."

"Lovely meeting you, Meg. Yes, I give private lessons. Group lessons are much more fun, though," Kemsit explained.

"I'm sure they are, but I would like to begin with private lessons. I'm not into performing."

"Are you sure?"

The way she asked, made Meg tremble. There was no way that this woman would know who she was. Was there? She hoped not.

Meg cleared her throat. "I'm sure."

"Are you new in town?"

"Yes, I left a bad relationship." Meg had to think fast. "I'm a waitress at the Belle Diner."

Kemsit chuckled. "Ah, men. The Belle is a nice place to work. I know the owner. She was student, until her business took over her life. You will like it there. Here, let me show you around the studio."

The dance studio was larger and prettier than any she encountered in L.A. In a small town, the rent had to be much more reasonable. Meg was impressed with the beverage bar and boutique. Mention shopping, and she was on it. Already, she selected, and purchased a coin hip scarf, in shocking pink. Kemsit showed her the office, and handed her a brochure. Meg eagerly filled out the application, and paid for her first session of lessons, and arranged for a time to meet.

"Private lessons are one hour in length. I like to begin with the basics, to assess your abilities," Kemsit explained.

"I'm sure that I will need to start at the beginning. It's been a few years since I had time for lessons, and I'm rusty."

"I will make sure that the rust melts away." Kemsit's smile was bright and wide. She possessed and honest warmth, that was reassuring.

WHEN MEG RETURNED to her apartment, to get ready for work, she felt good about her decision to take a sabbatical, and land in Cairo. Just like the dance class, she was returning to the basics.

3

M eg was getting back into the waitressing mode. Like riding a bike, navigating crowded booths and counters, while balancing laden trays of food and drink, returned like second nature. Instead of being fearful of not doing a good enough job, and getting fired, this go-round was actually fun. She delighted in serving her customers. Waiting on others, instead of always being waited on, gave her personal satisfaction. It was like giving back to society. Not needing the money, also added to her confidence. Of course, her boss and co-workers viewed her as a struggling single woman.

The clanging of pans, clinking of glasses, and the greasy scent of the grille was music to her ears, and a strange perfume. She found it all rather comforting. The atmosphere brought back memories of her teen years, when she was a struggling actress. Waitressing paid for the seedy motel room where she lived, and the acting lessons she scrimped and saved, to take. There was comfort in the familiar.

She was setting down two hamburger platters at a booth with two young women. The magazine one of the women was sharing, caught her attention. The image inside was that of a glamorous Marilyn Monroe-like woman, draped in fur and diamonds. Her platinum hair was fluffy, and flirty. A come-hither look was in her deep blue eyes. Her makeup was strik-ing, and her cleavage rather pronounced.

"Daphne is my favorite actress. She has it all; beauty, talent, and wealth," the woman gushed.

"Yeah, some women have it made. Lucky her," the other woman replied.

Lucky her? If they only knew. Meg cleared her throat, and smiled.

"Thank you," the women replied, ignoring her.

Meg walked toward the kitchen with her empty tray, ready to fill another order. Funny, when you're normal, you are invisi-ble. How ironic. Her alter ego, Hollywood persona, Daphne, was at their table, and without the accouterments of fame, the women didn't notice.

LATER THAT EVENING, as she lay on her living room sofa, that doubled as a bed, Meg thought about how she had walked away from a $25-million film contract to go find herself. She had been working nonstop for ten years, and was facing burnout. Her agent had a fit when she announced that she was going on an open-ended sabbatical, place unknown. Didn't she know that sex symbols in Hollywood had an expiration date? In a few years, she would be begging for plum roles. Didn't she know that she had to strike while the fire was hot? She was a leading lady, the most bankable actress on the planet, an A-lister, and at the top of her game.

"Come on, Les," she said. "I'm not retiring. I'm just taking a little break."

"Why, now? Finish this film. The role was made for you. I don't know if I can have them delay production."

"You said that last time, and another film came about, and another. I'm not a machine. I need some time off, or I will go insane."

"Do you want some other ingenue to replace you?"

She sighed. They had this argument before. She knew that she was in her prime, the industry's "flavor of the month," until a younger bombshell appeared.

The memory seemed so long ago. Yet it had only been a few weeks.

Money. He was concerned about money. It was always about money. Her agent would be missing out on his cut of the movie advance, and profit, if the producers couldn't wait for her. He didn't need the money. She didn't need the money. She had amassed enough of a fortune to live comfortably, and in the lap of luxury, for the rest of her life. Funny, she thought that money would bring her happiness. All it did was purchase security.

Being a glamorous and famous film actress had been her dream since childhood. The reality was far different. Being fussed over and worshipped was over-rated. Those who hired her, and those she hired only saw her as screen goddess, Daphne. Daphne generated a profit. In greedy Hollywood, that's all that mattered. Daphne was a golden goose. No one cared to know Margaret "Meg" Miller.

MEG MET WITH KEMSIT, at her studio, at the appointed time. She had worn stretchy black yoga pants, a baggy tunic, and tied the hot pink hip scarf at her hips. Kemsit wore a black catsuit, with mesh at the midriff, and a zebra-print coin scarf at her hips. It was ironic how Kemsit was beautiful enough for Hollywood, while she resembled the hired help.

"We will start with stretches to warm-up," Kemsit began.

Meg followed her every move. With every crack and pop, she knew that she was out of shape.

Kemsit progressed to dance moves.

"We will begin with basic arm movements. I'm sure that you will remember these," Kemsit explained, beginning with snake arms.

"Oh, yes," Meg said, following the flowing, shoulder-elbow-wrist movements. She always felt like a bird flying, when she created the full, and half snake motions.

"It is like riding a bike, no?" Kemsit smiled.

"Yes, some things do come back."

"You are very graceful."

Meg chuckled. She had been told by producers that she was elegant and graceful in her movements, and walk. Supposedly, it had added to her sex appeal.

"We shall progress to front snake arms, leaning back, and then reaching up, to add dimension and interest," Kemsit said, demonstrating the fluid movement.

Meg followed. She continued to follow Kemsit's example and instruction, as they progressed to head, rib cage and hip movements. The beginner moves came back, and Meg found comfort in the familiar.

"You're very good," Kemsit commented, "a natural dancer."

"Thank you."

"Other than taking belly dance classes, have you taken other dance classes?"

Hesitating, Meg answered, "A little ballroom."

She couldn't explain how she had intensive ballroom dance lessons in preparation for an acting role requiring the ability to waltz. That was several years ago, for a part that garnered her an Academy Award for Best Actress in a leading role.

"Are you sure you aren't interested in performing in the future?"

Shaking her head, Meg answered, "No, I'm really quite shy."

"Maybe I can convince you?" Kemsit winked.

Meg smiled. Little did Kemsit know, that she had been a born performer. She had been born and raised in the middle of nowhere. Her father was one of a myriad of men her mother had sex with. A mentally unstable drug addict, her mother grew up, and lived on public assistance, in public housing, moving to inner city Chicago when Meg was a preteen. Meg was raised like a weed, fending for herself. She created fantasy worlds in her mind, to escape the poverty, and to cope. She was a voracious reader, and dramatized the stories.

After class, she strolled back to her apartment. There was a chill in the evening air, and the streets were quiet. She cherished the quiet. So much of her life was filled with chaos and noise. The streets where she grew up were littered with trash, and people that society threw away.

Her mind wandered to her past, and her teen years. Unlike her siblings, she had longed to escape the mean streets and subsidized life. She loved school, and learning. At school, she was just another student, not a vagabond. She fit in, though she ate her only meal of the day, a subsidized lunch. In school, she absorbed drama classes, and did well. In high school, she won the lead in all-school plays. She dreamed of college after graduation.

Her hopes of a scholarship vanished, when her mother's latest lay placed his hands on her budding breasts. She had inherited her mother's assets. When that seedy, greasy man, who was old enough to be her grandfather touched her, with lust in his steely eyes, she knew that she had to leave. Being raped wasn't in her plans. She was not going to end up like her older sisters, all unwed mothers, living on welfare, in Section 8 housing. Before the man could grope her, she darted out of the apartment. She raced past the dank halls, with urine-saturated carpet and dark stairwells, into the fresh outdoor air.

She didn't know where she was going. School had just let

out for the summer, before her senior year. No stranger to the streets, she was streetwise. She did not plan on turning to a life of crime, as had her friends, nor was she going to join a gang as a family substitute. She knew that her mother and siblings wouldn't miss her. They were too strung out to notice, or care. No one would care if she lived or died. Swiping back tears, she was determined to succeed in life, without getting eaten up by the streets.

Getting a night shift, in a 24/7 restaurant, and sleeping under trees in a desolate park during the day, she saved enough cash for a one-way bus ticket to L.A. Being a waitress saved her. Funny, it was saving her again.

4

R utherford Rutledge was a modern business tycoon. Unlike the Robber Barons of old, his success and wealth came from the technology field. His firm, R&R Technologies, was the international leader in the development and implementation of Artificial Intelligence (A.I.).

While most tech firms were located in Silicon Valley, his was in the rural Midwest. Just like himself, it was a nonconforming outlier. Most of the people in the communities where he had facilities, had no idea as to the depth and reach of his enterprise. He eschewed being a member of the Chamber of Commerce, Rotary, Lions, or other civic organizations. He and his businesses operated in relative obscurity.

He avoided the trappings of wealth and success. His awards and proclamations were locked in his headquarters' office, as were the diplomas for his advanced degrees and professorships. A self-made nerd, he didn't flaunt his success. To the contrary.

Driving a beater car, he dressed like the farm guys in the community. His old farmhouse was set back in the middle of rural acreage, hidden from view. Instead of raising crops, or tending to animals, he tinkered with technology. The big red barn on his property housed his "think tank," where he hosted retreats for top scientists, who shared their latest discoveries and research on A.I. His motto was, "Once a geek, always a geek."

Within the local community, he had few friends. Those he did have were loyal. They never disclosed his private life, or the magnitude of his business. Thus, he lived in the community as just another low-key, blue collar worker.

He had favorite places to eat. Between The Coffee Cup Bistro in Cairo, and the Belle Diner, his dietary needs were met. Not one to cook, he preferred home-style food, eaten out. One of his favorite lunch places was the Belle Diner.

On a bright spring day, he ambled in to the Belle.

"Hey, Shelley, how's it going?" he greeted the owner.

She smiled with familiarity. "It's going."

He found a stool at the counter, his favorite place to sit. Coming in after the lunch crowd afforded some privacy and space.

"Customer," Shelley yelled back into the kitchen.

A tall, attractive woman, her mousy hair tied back in a ponytail, emerged from the kitchen. Attired in black slacks and a white tunic, she carried a menu. As she handed it to him, he recognized her.

"It's Meg from the Bistro," he greeted. "Remember me? River."

She met his gaze, with a tilted head.

Smiling, she said, "My dinner partner."

"One and the same."

"Well, today I'm your server."

He took the menu, and opened it. "I preferred it the other way around."

"Today's special is the meatloaf, with real mashed potatoes, and fresh green beans. It comes with a side of coleslaw," she said, in her lilting voice.

He closed the menu and handed it to her. "I'll take it. Add a chocolate milkshake, with real ice cream."

"Of course." She chuckled.

He watched her sashay to the kitchen. What a pleasant surprise. He had forgotten that she told him that she was a server. What was such an intelligent, pretty, and wholesome young woman doing, working in a diner in the middle of nowhere? He remembered how she had said that she left a bad relationship, and was living in Cairo. There seemed to be more bad relationships in the world, than good ones these days.

Instead of being honest in dating, people tended to play games. They always seemed to be looking for something. In his case, it was materialistic. The women he met, always seemed to be sizing him up by his attire, his job, and the car that he drove. No one wanted to spend the time to get to know him as a person. A bank account seemed more important that his intelligence, ideas, opinions, beliefs, morals, and his heart. By coming across as blue-collar poor, he was rarely given that chance.

When Meg returned with his meatloaf platter and milkshake, she set it down in front of him.

"Thanks. Can you join me?" he asked.

She shook her head. "I'm working. I can't fraternize with the customers."

"I see." Out of the corner of his eye, he could see Shelley in the corner, looking out for her employee, like a mother hen.

"Enjoy your lunch," she said with a smile, and walked away, toward Shelley, and the kitchen.

∾

MEG WAS SURPRISED to see the handsome stranger seated at the bar stool in the diner. Shelley had informed her that he was a regular customer.

"Treat him nice. He tips well," Shelley said.

Meg nodded. She didn't tell her boss that she had already met River, at another restaurant.

She was impressed that he acknowledged their prior meeting with an eager smile, and enthusiasm. When he had asked her if she could join him for lunch, she thought that it was a kind gesture. His invitation seemed genuine. It had been years since she could trust any man to be honest.

Men viewed her as Daphne, the sexy, seductive actress. They only wanted her as arm candy for photo-ops, and to get her in bed as a fun conquest. Daphne was viewed as a play thing. No one wanted Meg.

She sighed. Her life revolved around acting, portraying fictional characters on stage and screen. As Daphne, she was acting like a kittenish sex object. Yet, in reality, she was really just old-fashioned Meg.

In Cairo, and at the diner, she could be Meg. Though she was supposedly acting, hiding her identity as Daphne, she wasn't acting at all. Meg was the person she really was, beneath all the glamour and glitter. To be accepted as Meg meant more to her than the Oscars that sat on a shelf in her ostentatious mansion.

She observed River eating his lunch, from the dish pass-through in the kitchen, that she was wiping down. He had manners that would make Emily Post proud. Just because he was a tow motor operator, did she think that he would be crude? Heck, some famous actors ate like wild animals on a kill.

A couple of customers entered the diner, and Shelley seated them. Meg handed them menus, and after, wrote their orders.

Halfway through River's meal, she made an appearance to ask him if everything was to his liking.

"The meatloaf is incredible. There's so much here, that I doubt if I'll be needing dinner."

She smiled. "That's good to hear."

"Are you having a good day?" he asked.

"So far, so good." Out of the corner of her eye, she could see Shelley watching her. "Do enjoy the rest of your lunch. If you need anything, just wave."

She went back to the kitchen to set platters of food on her tray, to deliver to the other customers.

Passing Shelley, she whispered, "He loves the meatloaf."

After River was done eating, she approached to clear his dishes.

Placing them on a tray, she asked, "Would you be interested in dessert. Today's homemade pie is banana cream."

He met her gaze, with twinkling emerald eyes. "I'd love a slice. Now, I definitely won't be needing dinner."

"Good choice. You won't regret it."

She went to the refrigerated dessert display case to retrieve a slice of pie. She returned to hand it to him, with a clean fork and napkin.

"Thanks."

She turned to leave.

"What's your favorite pie?" he asked.

She faced him. "French Silk. Why?'

"I just wondered." He took a bite of the pie. "Tell Shelley that no one bakes better pies than she."

"I will."

She told Shelley, who made one of her "Oh, shucks," smiles.

The other customers were finished eating, so she visited their booths. They weren't interested in dessert, so she presented them with their checks. She noticed that River was done with his pie, so she took his plate, and handed him his check.

"Thanks," he replied. "Everything was wonderful, including

the service." He winked. His words made warmth permeate her body. Being appreciated for doing something as humbling as serving, meant a lot.

The other customers had gone to the register to pay Shelley for their food. She went to bus their tables, and retrieve her tips. The tabs were around $25 per couple, and the tips $4.00, typical 15%. When she turned around, River was gone. She felt bad that he had left without saying goodbye.

With a sigh, she went to the counter to pick up his dishes and such. Money was folded and neatly placed under his water glass. Next to it, was a note scribbled on a clean napkin.

"Dinner, Friday night, seven o'clock. Same place we met. Be there," it read.

His words brought a smile to her face. She placed the napkin in the pocket of her apron. She lifted the water glass to get her tip. He had left a $10 tip, quite generous for a $15 meal.

Shelley walked by, and chuckled. "Told you he was a good tipper."

5

Meg was contemplating what to wear for her meeting with River at the Bistro Friday evening. She got off work at four, showered, and washed her hair. Reading his note at least a dozen times, she kept asking herself if this was a date. If it was, what the hell was she doing? She disappeared to find herself, not a boyfriend.

This was deception. Yes, her legal name was still Margaret Miller, but to the world, she was Daphne. What if this became serious? How would he react when he found out that she was the world's most famous sex symbol, in disguise? Would he think that he hit the jackpot, and begin to treat her like all of the other opportunistic men who thought they hit pay dirt, dating her? Would he be upset that she lied, and walk away from her, and the baggage of fame? Why take a chance, if it could lead to heartbreak?

Yet, a little voice in her head told her to "take a chance." Heck, she did "take a chance, dance." Wasn't romance a dance?

She realized that if she wore cosmetics, and fluffed up her hair, she would look a little too much like Daphne. Maybe he wouldn't notice the resemblance, but someone surely would.

Never in her life had she gone out a date without makeup. Wearing her hair straight and limp, she resembled the nerdy girl that she was in high school. As for clothes, anything that enhanced her statuesque proportions was out of the question. Attracting unwanted attention was not her goal. She chose black leggings, and a long, baggy floral tunic. No jewelry. She had left her good stuff locked in her safe back home, anyway.

When she looked in the mirror, she wondered how any man would ever ask for a second date, by her appearance. She definitely was not Daphne.

RIVER LOOKED at his watch for the third time. She was late. At least he hoped she was just late, and not standing him up. Asking her out to dinner was on a whim. There was something about Meg, that was mysterious. She intrigued him, and he wanted to know her better. The question was whether she wanted to know him better. Tow motor operators were not exactly good catches to most women, at least in his experience. Not that he was expecting to be caught.

When she sauntered into the restaurant, being led to his table by the hostess, he stood to greet her. He grinned with the knowledge that she took him up on his invitation. Meg looked lovely. Unlike most women who were over-the-top, with cosmetics and hair styles, she was fresh scrubbed and wholesome. Her ivory complexion was clear and radiant, with just a hint of natural blush on her cheeks, and her lips a subtle rose. Straight brown hair framed her face nicely. Her eyes were glittering aquamarine. Her legs were thin and shapely. The tunic was pretty, but hid most of her body. Her figure was an interesting mystery. Though she was pretty, he was more attracted to her mind, and person. He was not a man who lusted after bodies, but brains. Though she was a waitress, he suspected that she was far more intelligent than the profession required. At least she gave that impression.

"Hi, sorry I'm late," she said.

"Better late than never," he replied, going over to her chair, and pulling it out for her. After, he went back to his seat, across from her.

"To what do I owe this invitation?" she asked, meeting his gaze.

The baby blue of her eyes held depth and power. He grew suddenly warm, and took a sip of water.

A server appeared with a glass of water for her, and two menus. River took one menu, and handed the other to her.

"I had such a delightful dinner with you last time, that I decided it needed an encore," he explained.

Was she blushing? He hadn't seen a woman blush since high school.

"So, how is your new life treating you?" he asked.

"I'm adjusting. It's become rather routine, with serving at the Belle, dance classes at Kemsit's, and the convenience of Cairo."

"You're studying with Kemsit? She's an interesting person, and I've heard that she's a very good instructor. She's an amazing dancer. I'm sure she'll invite you to one of her student showcases, and maybe even get you to perform in one."

"I take private lessons. Though I'd love to see her dance, I am not a performer. I'm too shy." She lowered her gaze.

"Kemsit has a way of bringing people out of their shell. Never say never."

A waitress appeared for drink orders.

"Amy, a Chardonnay for the lady, and ..."

"A Guinness on tap?" the waitress added.

He nodded, and she left to get their drinks.

"You know everyone?' Meg asked.

"Only at restaurants," he replied. "Amy happens to be the sister-in-law of my best friend."

"I see."

"By the way, if your car ever needs a repair, my friend, Luke, at Luke's Auto Garage is the best mechanic around."

"I've walked by that shop. I'll make a note of it."

"Cairo is a small town, and people tend to know one another."

"I get that impression."

The waitress brought their drinks. River watched Meg sip her Chardonnay, her delicate hand holding the glass as if it were fine crystal.

Setting down her glass, she asked, "So, you know about me. I don't know about you. What is your routine?"

He hesitated. "I'm rather boring. I just work, and tinker around my house. As you've probably surmised, I don't like to cook."

She chuckled in a low, sultry manner. "I've surmised."

"I'm a bit of a techno geek. I find technology fascinating," he said, knowing that it was an understatement.

"Fascinating and scary," she answered.

"Why, so?"

After taking a sip of wine, she said, "Well, technology has changed our way of life, and society in so many good ways. From communication to medicine, it has enhanced our lives, and made things so much more efficient. Yet, it is taking the humanity out of humans."

He stared at her. Interesting. He leaned forward. "How so?"

"Technology is taking the place of human interaction. I mean, from robots in factories and even in surgery, to self-checkouts and kiosks, we are dealing with machines, instead of people. Ordering everyday needs on the computer are causing stores to close. People are losing jobs. Efficiency and making money are replacing the personal touch. One day, are we to just sit in front of a computer to do everything? I mean, you can order everything you need, even pets and dates, on a screen."

He chuckled. "You think that artificial intelligence is a bad thing?"

"It's a mixed bag. People spend too much time in front of screens, as it is. Heck, people jog while looking at their phones. They can't even enjoy nature, and the beauty around them."

"And, they have walked into poles, and fallen off cliffs."

"Exactly."

"How has technology enhanced life?"

She pondered. "Well, in the film industry, it has made set design and special effects so much more dynamic, and real. Instead of thousands of extras and massive sets, computer generation has saved time and money. It has enhanced the movie viewing experience."

"I take it that you like movies?"

She finished her wine in one gulp. "I ... I am a fan."

The waitress came to the table, and they placed their orders. After she left, River took a sip of his Guinness, and met Meg's glittering gaze.

"You are a fascinating woman," he commented, meaning it.

She shrugged. "I don't know about that."

"Most women I've known, have had little to say about technology."

"I like to read, and learn about things."

"So, where did you relocate from?"

"Um ... California."

"No wonder you like the movie industry. L.A.?"

"Nearby."

"It's a long way from L.A. to Cairo."

"Tell me about it."

"Must have been a bad breakup?"

"Huh?"

"You had mentioned it when we met."

"Oh." She fidgeted in her seat.

He shook his head. "Sorry, I won't mention it again. I won't pry."

"I like it here." She raked a hand through her hair.

"I do, too." He did. Little did she know that he had lived in California for a bit, resided in San Francisco, and even worked in Silicon Valley. He preferred small town America to the big city, and corporate rat race. He did travel to L.A. a few times a year for business.

Their food arrived, and they focused on eating.

After dinner, he walked her down Main Street. The frosty globes on the antique lamp posts emitted a subtle glow, a full moon illuminating the sky. The Victorian storefronts and brick inserts in the pavement added to the small-town ambiance.

"The breeze smells like rain," River said, inhaling the cool evening air.

"You think?"

He nodded. "In a few hours. You can bank on it."

"I guess we have good timing."

"Thank you for an interesting evening," he said. "I enjoyed discussing technology with you."

Her smile was sparkling.

"I do like more than small talk," she said.

So did he. Most women he dated tended to spend the evening talking about themselves, or their jobs, and accomplishments.

"Well, this is where I live." She pointed up to a bay window, overlooking The Classy Chassis, where a brass lamp was lit.

"Cute and convenient."

"It really is. Thank you for a lovely evening." She put out her hand.

He took her hand, lifted it to his lips, and kissed it. "Thank you."

She smiled, tilting her head.

He liked that she was old-fashioned. No kisses, or more on a first date.

"Enjoy the rest of your evening," he said, releasing her hand. He turned to walk away. His car was parked near the restaurant.

"Good night," she said.

He half-turned, and blew her a kiss. "Good night."

6

"Let's work on our choreography," Kemsit said.

Meg had been taking private lessons for several weeks, and was surprised at how much she had retained from her earlier classes in California. Kemsit added new movements and props to the mix. A short choreography was also on the agenda.

Though she spent hours on her feet at the diner, dancing was different. Dance was an escape from reality. The intricate movements added grace and flexibility. Controlling her muscles was empowering. A raw sensuality was released. As crazy as it seemed, she had been the world's top sex symbol, yet faked it. Being sensual and sexy had been an acting gig. Dancing made it real and earthy.

"Got your sexy back?" Kemsit asked, startling her. How did Kemsit know?

Meg laughed. "Back? Did I ever have it?"

Kemsit winked. "My guess is that you have. It's just been too long."

Meg listened to Kemsit, and followed her examples. When the music began. She waited, as Kemsit had advised, "A dancer should have an aura of mystery. Music playing before the dancer appears, prepares the audience for something special. At the drumbeat, she makes her entrance, wrapped in a veil, playing finger cymbals. while prancing about."

As the music slowed, Meg removed the veil, one section at a time. Not a striptease, just a tease. Bare a shoulder, reveal a hip. Veil dancing involved dance movements, while swirling, folding, wavering, and tying the chiffon veil. The veil became an extension of her being, like an extra appendage. Tossing the veil to the floor, the music slowed, yet again.

"Hiss," Kemsit hissed like a snake, as a reminder to slow it down.

Time for undulations and belly rolls, figure eights, and other slow and sensuous moves.

As the music became more vibrant, the pace quickened, and her moves became more joyful. A build-up with the drums, she swirled around in circles, before dropping to the floor in a finale.

Kemsit applauded with *zhagareets*.

Meg, sat. "Phew. That was quite a workout."

"You were in the zone, and your dance was mesmerizing."

"Thank you. I really was in the zone." Being in the zone was something all performing artists strived for. It was that private moment, when everything disappeared around you, save for your art. It was as if you were alone with yourself.

"Me and my dance companies are performing a student showcase at the King Tut in a couple of weeks. I wish that you would consider performing."

Meg shook her head. She had heard about the exotic Middle Eastern restaurant, with the stage. "Oh, no."

"I'd like to see you ditch those long tunics, let your hair down, put on a cabaret costume, and dance. You have the talent." Kemsit placed her hands on her hips.

"I prefer not to be on display."

"There will be many dancers. You don't have to have to worry about being recognized."

The comment lent her pause.

Meg stared at Kemsit. "Who would know me here?"

"Exactly," Kemsit said with a laugh. "Think about it. After the show, there is a *hafla*, a party, and you can bring a guest. There will be a food buffet, and dancing all night. You can meet other dancers, and members of my dance companies. It will be fun."

MEG THOUGHT about Kemsit's invitation. She didn't become Hollywood's A-list actress by sitting back and being shy. Though a quiet loner by nature, she had trained herself to become an extrovert, regarding her career. Meg was a plain, bookish nerd, who rarely dated or partied, and preferred her nights alone. Her persona, Daphne was the glamorous and vivacious actress who shined in the spotlight. Cairo was a small town, and the least likely place anyone would expect to see the famous Daphne. Heck, she didn't even resemble the bombshell. Well, maybe her figure did, but other women, especially belly dancers, had fabulous figures. No one would put two and two together. While studying with Kemsit, she had the idea of doing a feature film, where she belly-danced, now that she had the ability. This could be sort of a dress rehearsal. The idea had actually made her feel renewed, and excited about returning to Hollywood, and her acting career. Take a chance, dance.

MEG THOUGHT that the King Tut belonged in Hollywood, not in a small town in the middle of nowhere. The exterior, with its gilding and pharaoh theme could have been created by studio set designers. The interior resembled the set of a kitschy classic

Biblical film. All it needed was Charlton Heston. The Egyptian murals on the walls, and bas relief near the stage were bright and colorful. The floor pillows and low tables added a harem look. Yes, she thought, belly dancers would certainly add to the atmosphere.

She carried her dress bag and tote across the stage to find the dressing room. Band members dressed in long, jewel-toned tunics were unpacking their instruments. She recognized the oud, riq, and doumbek. This place was authentic. Even the air held the scent of cinnamon and cardamom.

After having viewed a tutorial on You-Tube, she had applied her stage makeup at her apartment, so all she had to do was don her costume and accessories for the show. She tried to look more Middle Eastern, than Daphne. With the cosmetics and long, mousy hair, she hardly recognized herself when she looked in a mirror. Mission accomplished.

"Hi," a pert voice greeted, as she entered the dressing room.

Meg turned to face a cute blonde, with aquamarine eyes, lined with glitter.

"Hi."

"You must be Kemsit's latest discovery," the woman said, with a smile, putting out her hand. "I'm Emily, or Javairea, an old discovery."

Meg shook her hand, noticing the mystical henna tattoo. "Nice meeting you."

"So, we are the soloists, along with Kemsit, tonight."

"It's the first time I'm belly dancing in public," Meg admitted.

"A little fear, and adrenaline rush are good things. When you get on stage, they turn into energy. You will forget you are even on stage."

"The zone?"

Emily nodded. "Exactly. Kemsit knows what she's doing.

She is like a talent scout. She'd never throw just anyone on stage."

"That's good to know. The first time doing anything is scary."

"If it will make you feel better, this is my first time on stage in over a year. I had a baby, and was on break," Emily said.

"Congratulations."

"Thanks, I also had to fit in a costume, again."

The dressing room filled with members of Kemsit's dance companies, and the chatter intensified. There were a mix of married and single women, young and older, and different ethnicities. Meg met other ladies, and found them to be cordial. Unlike actresses she had worked with, these ladies were friendly and fun. They even helped her don her costume. Kemsit found her a barely-worn Bella, with *bedlah*, skirt, armlets, jewelry, and a silk veil. The blue and fuchsia floral print was striking. Unlike her Hollywood experience, the women were devoid of petty jealousy and drama. She sensed that dance was a hobby for most, and that they danced for joy. Funny, when serious money was involved, attitudes changed. She was grateful for the sense of joy.

When Kemsit entered, the atmosphere turned serious. Meg noticed that it was getting closer to showtime. The women primped in front of lit mirrors. The scent of perfume wafted in the stuffy room, along with anxiety and jitters. Glittering costumes were donned, and Meg felt strangely at home. The scene reminded her of the stage, when she was part of the cast of a Broadway play. She hadn't felt such anticipation in years. The memories this scene brought back were welcome. Maybe she needed to go back, in order to move forward.

"You have an enviable figure," Sara, a fellow dancer commented, as she helped her with her veil.

"Thanks." Meg glanced at her reflection in a full-length mirror, and Daphne stared back.

"Perfect for belly dance." Sara winked.

What the heck was she doing?

BACKSTAGE, Meg peered out into the audience. Somewhere out there was River. At least she hoped that he had had taken her up on her invitation to join her for the show, and party after. The band was playing prelude music, priming the audience for the performers.

Kemsit appeared in the wing. Her gold and white chiffon costume was ethereal, the gossamer veil draped around her. The color offset her caramel skin and long, black hair. Her Egyptian beauty was accented with dramatic cosmetics, and her glittering sapphire eyes. She posed, with her zills, finger cymbals, in mid-air.

With the drumbeat as her cue, Kemsit pranced on the stage, like a queen in her element. With zills tinkling, she garnered the audience's rapt attention. Their gaze never wavered, as she proceeded to command the stage. Fast steps and shimmies led to a slow and methodical removal of her veil. As the *taxsim* music slowed things down a notch, she descended to the floor with a backbend. Snake-like undulations and vibrations, with slinky figure-eights brought gasps from the audience. A corkscrew move brought her to her feet. As the music's pace quickened, she danced a spirited *Karsilama*. She stepped down the stairs to dance among the crowded tables, to hand-clapping and *zhagereets*. Back on the stage, she spun, and dropped sideways to the floor. Thunderous applause erupted.

After, Emily whispered to Meg, "I have to follow that?"

Meg's pulse quickened. She had to follow that amazing performance, too.

Before Emily danced, Kemsit's student dance company entered the stage from both wings. With sparkling *baladi* dresses, adorned with coin hip scarves, and gilded canes, they performed a rollicking *raqs assaya*, cane dance.

Emily, as Javairea, appeared next. Her return to dance was an intricate drum solo, performed with her husband, Jordan, Kemsit's drummer. The handsome couple played off of one another. He drummed his doumbek, while she answered with hip and chest thrusts, undulations, and pops and locks.

Kemsit's professional dance company, Pharaoh's Daughters, followed, entering the stage waving, long, narrow fan veils. The ribbons of silk fabric had a life of their own. Accenting their hip movements, the fan veils rippled, circled their bodies, and billowed overhead. The constant motion was reminiscent of ocean waves, with the same power of mellow to tumult. The jewel tones of their cabaret costumes and swirling veils were mesmerizing.

Meg swallowed hard. She was next. Last, but not least. She had practiced long and hard for this moment. Her costume, with its vibrant colors and clear and colored crystals and beads shimmered in the overhead lights. The layered floral skirt, embroidered with crystals sparkled, and the armlets added a nice accent. She tied the tie-dyed veil to hide her costume, and create mystery. She hoped that the costume distracted from her statuesque figure. Unknown to the public, she was uncomfortable showing off her body. Getting out of her comfort zone had always been difficult, but worthwhile. She drew a deep breath.

The low beat of the doumbek was her cue. She drew another deep breath, as the exotic strains of the classic song, *Miserlou* began. She strode on the stage like a panther sizing up its prey. She accompanied her arm and hip movements with her zills. Her foot patterns, and intricate layering of upper and lower body became one with the music. She stalked all four corners of the stage. Her body took control, as she entered the "zone," dancing on air. Immersed in the music, she turned, removing part of her veil to expose a bare shoulder, and a hint of leg. Placing the veil as a backdrop behind her, dancing, she revealed her costume. The crystals and beads twinkled under the spotlight. Belly rolls and flutters brought gasps from the audience. Playing with the veil, she stepped down into the dining room, and pranced among the tables. Guests began to stand and shower her with money, the bills floating to the floor. Ignoring the cash, she continued dancing.

Meeting her gaze, were familiar emerald eyes, intense and radiant. River's facial expressions were a mix of grimaces and awe. He smiled, as she performed a rolling pelvic tilt to the drumbeat. When she draped her veil around his neck, his face turned crimson. She winked, before shimmying away. She smiled. He had come to see her dance. She danced with abandon and joy back on the stage. With a lively spin, she Turkish dropped dramatically to the floor. Rising, she smiled and curtsied. Performing was worth it, because River was there.

RIVER LOUNGED on a cushion at a low table, set in front of the raised stage. Meg had invited him to see her perform in the student showcase, presented by Kemsit. He had attended several showcases in the past. His best friend's wife performed in one of Kemsit's dance companies. The shows were professional and entertaining. None had surprised or enchanted him like this one. He had to give Meg credit for coming out of her shell. He also finally learned what Meg was hiding under those baggy clothes. When she removed her veil, she was an ivory goddess, with an hourglass figure of sensual curves. She was sexy as all hell. Who would have thought? Was it getting hot, or was he?

When she left the stage, he stood to applaud. He soon realized that the entire room was on its feet, as applause, whistles, and *zhagereets* erupted.

After the show, Meg appeared at his table. Though dressed

in leggings and a sparkly tunic, she still wore her dramatic stage makeup. River had to take a double-take. This femme fatale was wholesome Meg? She slunk on a floor cushion across from him.

"How did I do?" she asked.

He clapped, and slid a cool glass wine in front of her.

"I ordered you a Chardonnay. You deserve it, and more," he said.

She took the glass, and sipped. "You're right."

"You were amazing."

"Thank you. I'm glad you came."

"I couldn't miss it."

"Thank you."

"For someone who just started taking lessons with Kemsit, you are really good."

"Well, I studied in California a few years ago. Kemsit advanced my studies," Meg explained.

"You look and dance like a professional."

"You're being too kind. All of the dancers were wonderful."

"Yes, they were." He sipped his Guinness. "Hey, why were you hiding under all of those baggy clothes?"

"I don't like to draw attention to myself."

"And, you're from L.A.?" He laughed.

She stared at him. "What does that have to do with it?'

"I thought that all beautiful women in L.A. had acting ambition, and were attracting attention was part of the plan."

She took a sip of wine. If he only knew.

"I'm not in L.A., now," she said.

A waiter appeared, and announced, "The buffet is ready for your pleasure."

"Thanks. I guess that's our cue to grab dinner," River said, rising from his seat.

"Now I know why you really came tonight." Meg stood.

"Why?"

"Food. You couldn't miss a good meal."

River chuckled. "I think that you already know me too well. Actually, the main reason I came tonight, was to see you."

THE DINNER BUFFET was a delightful meal for the senses. River swore that the King Tut had the best array of Middle Eastern cuisine he had ever encountered, and tasted. He wasn't a gourmet when it came to food, but he appreciated it. Meg seemed to be surprised when he knew the difference between tabouli and baba ganoush. Food from different cultures always intrigued him.

Sitting on floor cushions, and dining with Meg, was enchanting. Her stage makeup made her resemble Scheherazade from The Arabian Nights. She went from being a natural beauty to an exotic knockout. The way she danced was sensuous as all hell, and her figure was incredible. Yet, he preferred the fresh-scrubbed, wholesome Meg, the waitress. Women who were physically beautiful, who were sexy and they knew it, were a dime a dozen. Decent women were not.

"You know, you are a mysterious contradiction," he said, holding a shish kebab skewer.

"I'm really quite shy." She sipped her wine.

"Tonight, you out-Kemsited Kemsit."

She laughed, shaking her head. "That would be impossible. I danced for fun, tonight."

"Well, thank you for inviting me to witness your transformation," he said.

She shrugged. "I'm the same Meg, just fancied up. After dinner, there will be dancing, if you like to dance."

"I'm not a candidate for "Dancing with the Stars," but I can try."

. . .

AFTER DINNER, River followed Meg to the stage. While the Arabic band played, the stage became a mosh pit for shimmying, undulating dancers and dancer wannabees. He tried to follow Meg's moves, but thought that he resembled someone being attacked by hornets. They shared laugher, and some intimacy during the slow dances. He fared better, holding her in his arms, and stepping slowly back and forth. Her sandlewood scent and gentle touch, set him off, and he pulled away to cool down.

River went to the bar to get some refreshing gingerale. He was holding two glasses, ready to return to Meg.

"Hey," a familiar male voice called.

River looked up. His best friend Luke appeared, with his lovely brunette wife at his side. They were holding glasses of wine.

"What brings you here, buddy?" Luke asked.

"A friend, who performed tonight, invited me," River answered.

"Friend, huh? This is interesting." Luke smirked.

"Who is she?" his wife asked.

"Meg. Meg Miller," River answered.

"Kemsit's private student. She's incredible. We met backstage," Sara said.

"That she is."

"The last dancer in the show?" Luke asked, with raised brows.

"One and the same."

"Wow."

Luke knew that he rarely dated, as River was known to be addicted to work.

"I'll introduce you," River said.

"This must be serious." River heard Luke whisper to Sara.

River turned to face his friend. "By the way, I'm a tow motor operator."

"Shh ..." Luke mused.

River led them to Meg, who was seated at the table, by the stage. She stood, and introductions were made.

"So, you own an auto garage in town?" Meg asked Luke. "River told me about you."

"I'm the *only* auto mechanic in town." Luke chuckled.

"You're a lovely dancer," Sara told Meg.

"Thank you. Kemsit is an amazing instructor, as you know."

"She truly is."

"She persuaded me to get on stage tonight," Meg said.

"Me, too."

"You're in her professional dance company, Pharaoh's Daughters."

Sara grinned. "I'm the newest member. I just got promoted from her student company."

"Wonderful."

"Hey, River, how did we luck out? Belly dancers." Luke winked.

Sara nudged Luke with her elbow. "He gets his fantasy a few nights a year."

AT MIDNIGHT, the crowd began to disperse.

"I'll have to grab my dance stuff from the dressing room," Meg said.

"I'll wait, and escort you to your car," River answered.

"I'd like that."

River thought that it was too bad that they drove separately. He would have enjoyed the extra moments of her company, if they had driven together. River had to admit that he had fun. For a person who preferred to stay at home alone, he actually enjoyed spending the evening with Meg, Luke and Sara, and the other dancers and their dates. The casual conversation was interesting. Meg added that special touch, with her joyful manner. He realized that he could never tire of her.

Meg was growing on him. She was charming, intelligent, and fun. Unlike most women he met, she didn't appear to have any motives or agendas. Considering that she had relocated to a new town, she seemed well-adjusted and content. Even her waitressing job seemed to bring her joy. No complaints or sob stories. She seemed to find happiness in everything.

He escorted her to her car in the parking lot. Putting her dance bag and tote in the passenger seat, he went to the driver's side, and opened the door for her. She drove an ordinary car, an old Ford Focus. He admired her ordinary and normal ways.

Standing next to the door, under a glowing full moon, she looked up at him with a glittering smile.

"Thank you for a delightful evening, and for walking me out," she said.

"It's getting late."

"I really liked your friends."

"Luke and Sara are great. We'll have to go out with them one night."

"I'd like that."

"This has been a special evening," River said, voice softening.

He met her gaze, as they stood under a parking lot lamp. The light illuminated her hair, and the shimmer of the stage makeup. The glow of her oval face mesmerized him. Her lips were full, parted, and enticing.

Without thinking, he cupped his hands around her face, and drew her up toward his. When his lips met hers, it was as if time stopped. An electrical warmth settled over him. The merging of lips was so magical and natural, a perfect fit.

She reached up with her arms, and encircled his neck in response. Kissing him back, the pressure of her lips had him drawing her closer. Another, deeper kiss brought a groan to his throat. He moved his hands and drew away. Brushing a strand of hair away from her face, he gazed at her. Never had he experienced such chemistry with a woman. The Earth stood still when he kissed her. He swore that it tilted on its axis.

"Thank you for making this evening special. I'm so glad you came," she whispered, and drew a deep breath.

"No, thank you for inviting me. You are an incredible dancer, and an even more incredible woman."

He took her hand, held it, and kissed it. Looking into her eyes was like touching her soul. His heart raced, and a soothing warmth permeated his body.

"Good night," he whispered

"Good night." She turned to get in her car.

"I'll wait for you to leave, to make sure your car starts, and you are safe," he said.

"I appreciate it, River. Good night."

7
___

River kissed her, and rocked her world. Meg was dancing on air. The chemistry was startling. For the first time in her life, she realized that she was falling in love. Love. That ever-elusive feeling had finally taken hold, and it took an average guy, with above average looks, to affect her.

"You blew them away," Kemsit said, when Meg floated into the studio for her lesson, after her debut performance.

"I don't know about that, but I got over $400 in tips."

"Maybe you found your calling? Better than waitressing?" Kemsit chuckled.

"I won't quit my day job. Performing was fun. If I did it all the time, it would become a job, and cease to bring joy." She thought of her acting gig.

"Regular jobs can do that. Being a performer, though, has its perks. You can pick and choose, and take a sabbatical, when needed. I return to Egypt, when I need to recharge," Kemsit said.

"You're from Egypt?"

Kemsit nodded. "Yes, and I've never forgotten my roots.

They keep me grounded. It's a good idea to return to one's roots, eh?"

Meg met her intense gaze, and it was if Kemsit could read her mind. Yes, Meg's escape to Cairo, had taken her back to the days when she was starting out. Back to the days when she was a waitress and struggling actress, before fame and fortune took away the dreams and the innocence.

Kemsit cleared her throat, and blinked. Looking away, she said, "Coming back, I always feel refreshed and motivated. I regain the joy of dance, and the creative energy returns in abundance. "

"It does," Meg muttered. She was feeling it. "Maybe we all need to escape our real life once in a while."

"You never know what, or who you will discover," Kemsit said, with a wink.

AFTER HER SHIFT at the diner, Meg returned to her apartment. Sitting on her sofa, she checked her cell phone. There was another message from Les. Her agent called regularly, trying to entice her back home.

Home. Where was home? Yes, she owned property in Hollywood, and had an established career there. Yet, she felt most comfortable in the little apartment above The Classy Chassis in downtown Cairo. She still hadn't finished furnishing or decorating it, and slept on the sofa, as the space was peaceful and comfortable. She could come and go as she pleased. If she wanted to stroll the streets at night, she could. No one was following her, photographing her, or asking for autographs. She was free. There was something to be said for being ordinary. She dialed Les.

"About time you called back," he answered.

"Well, gee, hello to you, too."

"Hello," he finally said in his gruff tone. Often, he sounded more like a father, than an agent.

"Have you finally gotten the burnout out of your system? Ready to come back?" he asked.

She laughed. "I'm getting there. Actually, I have a couple special requests."

"Special requests?"

"Yes. Being away has given me time to reflect. I'm tired of always playing the ditzy blonde bombshell. I'd like to get more roles with substance. I need to think about career longevity. I also need to expand my roles, to include more of my talent."

He chuckled. "Playing a blonde bombshell has made you rich. It never hurt Marilyn Monroe."

"Yes, it did. She ended up dead." She became serious.

He cleared his throat. "So, what do you suggest?"

"First, I'd like you to find some scripts about an intelligent woman, who performs Middle Eastern belly dance. Second, I'd like to return to the stage. I miss live theater, and the energy from a live audience."

He laughed. "An intelligent belly dancer? Sounds like an oxymoron."

"No. I've discovered that most dancers, hobbyists and professionals are educated women with advanced degrees, who have important careers."

"You're kidding, right?"

"No, I'm not. Think Mata Hari. Hey, now there's a character I can sink my teeth into. I can also dance."

"Greta Garbo did Mata Hari. There's also a Russian television series."

"I'm thinking, feature film. Very lavish and exotic."

"Would it lure you back here?"

"Hmmm. It just might."

"You do know that big director is still holding out for you. He can't delay production much longer."

"I get your drift."

"Promise me, and him, that you will come back to finish his motion picture, and I promise that I will get you your Mata Hari project. Hey, he might want to direct it. We can talk about live theater, later."

"You do know that you're making me offers I can't refuse."

"That's the idea," he said.

"You won't renege?"

"Have I ever?"

"No."

"Why would I start now?'

"Get me the Mata Hari project," she insisted.

"I will get right on it."

She smiled. Things were looking up. She thought about what Kemsit said about abundant creative energy. Portraying Mata Hari, and dancing would be an amazing role, that she couldn't wait to film. Then it hit her. She would have to leave Cairo for an extended period of time. Maybe, she could fly back to visit. What excuse could she make to preserve her anonymity? She knew, though, that once the Mata Hari project hit the screen, there would be no anonymity. Her appearance, and dancing would reveal her true identity. She had time to formulate a plan, and cross the bridge when she came to it.

MEG WAS INVITED TO A PARTY. Kemsit decided to host a *hafla*, a dance party, for the studio's dance companies and soloists. Being a pot luck, everyone was to bring something. Never having cooked or baked, Meg was perplexed. Being a small town, she was certain that the other women would be Martha Stewart personified. After her shift at the Belle Diner, she eyed the glass display case filled with baked goods. Shelley was renowned for her original-recipe pies and cakes. She selected a coconut cream pie, and a pistachio Bundt cake for the party.

When she arrived at the dance studio, the party was in full swing. Egyptian *Shaabi* music blasted from the corner speakers. Ladies, in street clothes, accented with coin hip belts, were holding plastic tumblers of wine and soft drinks. Rectangular folding tables, draped in red fabric were laden with a variety of casserole dishes, crock pots, and platters. She was balancing the cake and pie boxes, looking for a place to set them.

Kemsit glided in her direction.

"Let me help," Kemsit offered, taking the cake box. "Follow me."

She followed Kemsit to a corner, where a dessert station, and hot beverage service were set up. Kemsit removed the cake from the box and set it on the table amidst an assortment of cookies, brownies, lemon bars and eclairs. Meg, in turn, removed the pie from the box and set it down.

"What a perfect addition," Kemsit said, with a smile. She picked up a pie and a cake server from the utensil, plate, and napkin section, and took the box from Meg.

"I'll trash these. You go pour yourself some wine." Kemsit nodded toward a makeshift bar set up on a card table.

Meg ambled over to the bar, and poured herself some Chardonnay.

"You danced beautifully at the showcase," a perky blonde commented.

"Thank you."

"I'm Charise." She put out her hand, and Meg shook it.

"Meg. Do you dance in one of the companies?"

Charise nodded. "Yes, Pharaoh's Daughters. I just came back from maternity leave."

"I met Emily and Sara, who also had babies."

"Must be something in the water." Charise chuckled.

"I guess I'll have to stick to wine." She raised her glass.

"Dinner is served," Kemsit announced.

Meg lined up with the other ladies. For her, such a simple

act was fun. For so many years, she was first in line for every-thing, fawned over, and doted upon. She almost forgot how it felt to be ordinary.

She piled her plate with fried chicken, casseroles, vegeta-bles, a variety of salads, banana bread, and Jell-o mold. Comfort food was something she hadn't had in years. For the first time, she wasn't being guilted into eating light to maintain her slim frame. She was free to indulge.

Joining Charise at a round table, she recognized Emily, Sara, and Estelle. She was introduced to other dance company members. Some were in the beginner company, and others in Pharaoh's Daughters. All were fun and friendly.

Considering that they were performers, she wasn't expecting comaraderie. She had few friends in Hollywood. Ever since landing her first role, her life had been a whirlwind of auditions, filming, and promotion. She didn't have time for friends, and a social life. Her career was her life. Film was a cutthroat business, where people clawed their way to the top, not caring who they harmed in the process. An actress's career could be fleeting, or lifelong. Reinvention, strategic planning, leverage, and bringing in revenue were critical. Having a connected, competent, and honest agent was essential. Les was all three. She was determined to stick around, and worked hard to maintain her A-list position. After all, she was still on top, after ten years.

She knew that other actresses were out to dethrone her. They were silly, as each person was unique, and there were enough roles for true talent. You just had to embrace that role, and make it your own. As she glanced around the table, the women seated were all unique. Some were young, others older. They were different sizes, diverse ethnicities, unique faces, and expressions. Funny, this group of ordinary women, who embraced dance had the right attitude. They viewed each other as peers, not competitors.

"Do you audition to join the dance companies?" Meg asked.

Sara answered, "Kemsit has incredible intuition. By observing her students, she can determine their skill level, and where they belong. If she sees talent, she asks if the student is interested in joining a dance company, or being a soloist. The student determines whether or not they want to commit the time, and funds for extra training, group rehearsals, costuming, and performing."

"Sort of how she approached me."

"See, Kemsit is never wrong. You dance at a professional level, and belong on the stage," Emily added.

If she only knew.

Meg had a pleasant dinner with her new friends, who felt like old friends. Friends. She never had friends, or felt a part of a sisterhood before. She genuinely liked the group. By the end of the evening, they made plans to meet at Charise's home for an appetizer party in the near future. Sara also reminded her of a double date with Luke and River. Meg left with a warm and fuzzy smile on her face.

8

"Hey, River." Luke's voice reverberated on his cell phone."

"What's up?" He had just arrived at his office, and leaned back in his swivel chair.

"Just wanted to remind you that we're going out for Chinese tonight with Sara and Meg."

"Did you really think that I'd forget?" He chuckled, peering out of the glass wall at his sprawling tech campus.

"I know how you get hypnotized by work."

"Not when it comes to Meg."

"Hmm, this is sounding serious. It's not like you."

"There's something about her." He couldn't put it in to words.

"By the way, Sara really likes her. Kemsit hosted a party for her dancers the other night, and Meg fit right in."

"So, you're telling me that she's Sara-approved."

"You know that Sara is a great judge of character."

. . .

DINNER at the hole-in-the-wall Chinese restaurant was the perfect location for a casual dinner with friends, and suitable for a tow motor operator and an auto mechanic. River snickered. He donned jeans and a chambray shirt for the occasion. Meg was pretty in black leggings and a striped handkerchief-hemmed tunic. Luke and Sara were similarly attired. This was the first time he ever introduced a date to his friends and double-dated. Luke and Sara wouldn't stop smiling.

"This place may seem plain, but they have the best Hunan cuisine," Luke said, peering at his menu.

River didn't open his menu. Meg tilted her head, holding her menu.

River shrugged. "I'm a creature of habit. I order the same thing every time I visit."

Orders were taken, and tea served.

"Meg, you seem to be adjusting quite well to life in the slow lane, in Cairo," Sara said.

"I like it here. Life is simple, and peaceful."

"River told Luke that you're living in town."

Meg nodded. "In an apartment above The Classy Chassis."

"Oh my gosh. That's where I lived when I arrived in town." Sara almost leapt out of her chair.

"No kidding? I love it. It came partially furnished. I, especially, love the room with the African animal murals."

"I decorated it, and left the furniture."

Luke chuckled. "Small world."

"This is too funny," Meg said.

"You ladies have good taste," River added.

"They're out with us." Luke winked.

"Don't you just love small town life? It just grows on you." Sara said.

"I agree."

"You know, River, you should take her on a ride to Amish

country. The countryside is rural, with rolling hills, meadows, and quaint homesteads," Luke suggested.

"There are Amish around here?" Meg asked, with a gleam in her eyes.

"Sometimes, you'll see a buggy hitched in town, though they have their own village with shops, and some great family-style restaurants," Sara added.

"I've read about the Amish, and saw that classic Harrison Ford film, 'Witness.' I've never seen real Amish."

"Sounds like a plan," River said. He met Meg's gaze. He had been so immersed in business, that he never went to Amish country. His recreation consisted of eating out, working out in his personal gym, and puttering around with new technology in his barn. Luke was always badgering him about his narrow interests. Maybe, he did need to branch out, and do more. He knew what people said about all work, and no play.

"So, Meg, what do you like to do for fun?" Sara asked.

Meg hesitated. "I like to read, watch movies ... dance."

"I love movies, too," Sara said. "Mostly classics, though I do love romantic comedies. My favorite actress is Daphne."

Meg was sipping water, and choked on it. Her eyes grew wide, and River was concerned.

"You okay?" he asked, draping an arm around her shoulder.

"I'll be fine." Her lip trembled, when she smiled.

"I know, everyone thinks she's a dumb blonde, but she's a brilliant actress to play the part," Sara said, adding, "You know, you resemble her."

"Thanks. I'll take it as a complement," Meg replied.

"It is."

Luke squeezed Sara's shoulder. "You're a star in my book."

MEG LIKED RIVER'S FRIENDS. Though she thought that Sara almost blew her cover, everything went well. There was genuine warmth and a sense of belonging. Being with real people was a pleasant departure from the often too-phony Hollywood scene. For the first time in years, she wasn't an object, but a person. She could be herself, without the trappings of a Hollywood goddess. There was no need to put on her kittenish Daphne voice and act. No one expected it. She was back to being Meg, before Les discovered her, and molded her into the world's sex symbol. Over the course of ten years she had been transformed into a caricature. She desperately needed to rediscover herself. Coming to Cairo, she realized, saved her life.

Les called.

"You got your deal," Les said. "Finish the Mob movie, and your Mata Hari project is on. You just need to get back here."

"Thank you, Les." She made a loud kissing sound, "Moi."

"When are you coming back?" He sounded agitated.

"As soon as I arrange things here. Soon." She would have to create an excuse to leave Cairo for an extended period of time. The sick relative excuse? She could still talk to River, and her friends.

"Soon," he insisted.

Her two worlds were colliding.

THE DRIVE to Amish country was a diversion from the plans Meg had to make. The rolling hills of green pastures were pristine, with cows and horses grazing behind miles of fences. Red barns and silos stood as sentinels on sprawling farms. Whitewashed homes had wrap-around porches. A kaleidoscope of laundry fluttered in the breeze. Black buggies drawn by trotting horses, clip-clopped down the road. She observed the fresh-scrubbed faces of women, and the bearded men in straw hats. The scene harkened back to a less hectic and material past.

"I often think that they have the right idea," Meg commented.

"It looks lovely, but it's a hard life," River added.

"I guess that we all have our own definition of hard."

River pulled into the gravel parking lot of a farmer's market. His tires crunched to a halt.

"This is the place for farm-grown produce, and Amish baked goods," he said.

Bins of sweetcorn, tomatoes, and melons were outside the front door. Inside, were more bins of produce, jars of jellies and condiments, jugs of maple syrup, and a plethora of baked goods.

"The strawberry-rhubarb pie is to die for," River said.

A young Amish woman, in navy dress, apron, and bonnet, approached. Her eyes sparkled, and she smiled, "Hi, River."

"Hi. How are you today? I brought a friend."

She frowned upon seeing Meg.

"Two strawberry-rhubarb pies," he ordered.

After shopping in the market, he drove to the Swiss cheese factory, to observe how cheese was made, and to purchase a few blocks. After, it was browsing a flea market, housed in a large warehouse. Meg could have done some serious damage, but had to remind herself that she was a struggling waitress, with a meager budget. Dinner was at a family-style Amish restaurant. She indulged on fried chicken, stuffing with gravy, real mashed potatoes, fresh green beans, rolls with maple butter, and German chocolate pie for dessert. She knew that she'd have to crash diet back in L.A. The thought of going back, both excited her, and haunted her.

RIVER WALKED her up to her apartment, carrying her purchases from the produce market. She opened the door, and they stepped on the small patch of wood foyer. He scanned the space. The sofa, two chairs and table with the brass lamp had been Sara's purchases. He remembered, having helped Luke move her out, before they were married. From what he could tell, there was little else, save for the equipped kitchen. There were no personal touches, and it seemed strange to him.

"So, this is the infamous apartment," he said, taking the bags to the kitchen, and depositing them on the counter. The kitchen was pristine, as if never used. Either she never cooked, or was a clean freak.

"Thanks." She began taking things from the bags, and putting them away. He helped.

When he opened the refrigerator, it was essentially empty, except for some bagged salad and fruit. Apparently, she didn't cook. Working in a restaurant, he surmised, she didn't have to. Who was he to judge? He never cooked, but ate out every day.

After she was done, she led him from the kitchen, to the hallway. "I want you to see the animal room."

He followed her. There was a bathroom at the end of the hall. He peeked into a bedroom. Devoid of furniture, open suitcases lay on the floor, clothes and shoes sprawled about. Either she was a minimalist, or had less money than he thought.

He followed her to an empty room, where the walls had murals of African animals. There were giraffes, zebras, lions, monkeys, and exotic birds. She seemed enchanted by the space that was Rick's nursery.

"Isn't it cute?" she gushed.

"It is."

They exited, and went to the living room.

"Thank you for a special day. I learned a lot. I can see why you like the Amish. They sure know how to cook and bake." She stood, facing him.

"I know, and I love to eat."

She laughed, in her giggly, girlish way.

"I had fun, too. I don't get out as much as I should," he said. "I best be on my way."

She glanced up at him with those glittering blue eyes. He couldn't resist her charm. Cupping her face with his hands, he lowered his face to hers, and kissed her on the lips. There was something about her kiss, that sent pulses throughout his body. He grew warm. Drawing away, he thought it best that he leave. There would be plenty of time for more, at the right time, and the right place

9

The morning was like any other. Meg awakened, dressed in her work uniform, and ate a bowl of instant oatmeal for breakfast, before going to her shift at the Belle Diner. For someone who used to sleep until Noon, she found peace in awakening at 5A.M. She especially loved leaving at dawn, when the sun was rising gold, and a cacophony of bird song filled the dewy, morning air. Morning allowed her time to think and contemplate her day. Having to be at the diner for the busy breakfast shift was more a joy than a burden. She loved the hurried atmosphere, and the interesting clientele. Sometimes, River even showed up.

She descended the steep stairs leading from her apartment down to the sidewalk.

From the moment she pushed open the glass door, she knew that she had entered a scene she had longed to avoid. She gripped her purse in front of her, like a protective shield. Throngs of paparazzi and news media descended on her like hawks stalking prey. Questions were blurted out, voices shrill and muffled. Faces became a blur. Too stunned to react, she covered her face with her hands, while trying to back up into the safety of her stairwell. Yet, the pit of people prevented it. Uncontrollable tears dripped down her cheeks. This was so wrong.

How did they find her?

Parting the crowd like Moses parting the Red Sea, Les appeared, pushing toward her. Grabbing her by the arm, he led her through the mass of people toward a waiting stretch limousine. The shimmering black automobile seemed so out of place on quaint Main Street. Shoving her inside the back seat, he joined her, slamming the door shut. Cameras flashed, and fists pounded on the window. The car rocked.

"Go!" Les ordered the driver.

Meg gasped for breath, her heart racing. As the car moved, she could see faces gazing into the windows. Estelle's shocked reaction had her whimper. So much for anonymity. So much for leaving on her own terms. This was so wrong. What was wrong with free will?

She seethed at Les, "Why? Why did you come here?"

He shrugged. "I didn't have a choice. It was for your safety. The moment the story hit the media, I had to come and rescue you."

"I don't need rescuing."

"But you did. How else would you have escaped the crush of reporters? The moment the news leaked, they flocked here."

"How did they know I was here? Who tipped them off? I was so careful and discreet."

The car rolled down Main Street toward the highway.

"It seems that someone in your household staff tipped off a reporter. She followed you from your home, to the auto dealership, and here."

"A reporter followed me? Someone from my staff snitched?"

"Yep. The reporter kept tabs on you, from a distance, and wrote quite an expose. She took some incredible pictures."

"Expose? Pictures? How did she follow me, without my knowing?"

"She's good at her job. Quinn Morgan is one of the top investigative reporters in the world."

Meg drew a hand up to her head. A headache was coming on.

Les pulled a glossy magazine out from under the seat. *Our World* magazine, one of the top investigative media companies in the world.

"It's in all formats, and all over the internet and media," Les explained, handing her the print publication.

The headline on the color cover screamed, "Daphne's Best Performance." She gazed at the photograph of her in costume, dancing at the King Tut."

"You know, this publicity is priceless," Les said, with a smirk.

"No," she screamed. "This is an invasion of my privacy."

"You can run, but you can't hide. It's the price you pay for being a celebrity, I'm afraid."

"Even I deserve a private life."

"Sadly, when you sign up for fame and fortune, you sell your soul to the public."

Though she knew it was true, it was still a high price to pay. You work so hard to have your name become a household word. When it does, you long for privacy. Why couldn't she have it both ways?

"This isn't fair. It just isn't fair."

She opened the magazine to search for the article.

10

R iver was stunned. That was an understatement. He had heard about the media descending on Cairo, but when he saw the news headlines and photographs on the internet, he almost fell back in his office chair.

"What the hell?"

His girlfriend, the demure waitress Meg, was really the sexy Hollywood bombshell, Daphne? Daphne? How could it be? Meg and Daphne were polar opposites. Yet, here it was for the entire world to see.

"She was some actress," he muttered.

Before reading the article, the photographs caught his eye. Someone had taken a lot of care to go undercover to photograph her so discreetly. Talk about an invasion of privacy. For some reason, she had wanted anonymity, and that was rudely taken away. It was so wrong.

He was perplexed. On one hand, he felt bad for her secret having been exposed. On the other, he was angry. She lied. Was she ever going to tell him of her deception, or was she just going to disappear one day, after having had her fun?

Was Meg real, or just another acting role for a Hollywood icon?

Hollywood icon? The revelation was so startling that he had to catch his breath. He clicked on the featured photograph.

"Shit!"

Enlarged was the evening kiss by her car, after her King Tut debut performance and party. How dare that reporter invade their privacy by capturing such a personal, and intimate moment? She invaded his privacy. The caption really infuriated him.

"Reclusive techno-preneur, Rutherford Rutledge, of R&R Technologies fame and fortune, is Daphne's main squeeze."

"Shit, shit, shit." He clicked off the internet, and closed his laptop.

Not only were Meg's lies exposed, so were his. This was now personal. When Meg, Daphne, whoever she was, read the piece, as he was sure she would, she would discover that he was not a tow motor operator. His real identity was revealed. His face, and hers were flashed for all the world to see.

How could he be so angry at her deception, when he was equally as guilty? He was no more a tow motor operator, than she was a waitress.

His office assistant knocked, and entered his office. From her disheveled appearance, she was exasperated.

"Mr. Rutledge, the office is going crazy fielding calls, I.T. is breaking down, and the press has congregated outside the building. It's pure chaos. What are we to do? Helen, from Communications is trying to control the frenzy. She locked the doors behind her to keep everyone from barging in."

"If anyone can handle the press, it's Helen." He forced a smile, trying to act cool and collected, when he was neither.

"If I may say so, Sir, she is like a Gladiator facing hungry lions."

Did she actually say that with a straight face? He had to

suppress laughter. Helen was tough as nails, and an expert at crisis communications, but a Gladiator?

"I'll see what I can do to appease the press. Ignore everything, and everyone else."

"Yes, Sir."

He rose from his seat, as she rushed out of his office. This was pure insanity. What the hell did his personal life have to do with his business? Everything, apparently. Tucking his plaid flannel shirt in his jeans, he raked a hand through his unruly hair and made his way to the corridor elevator. Pushing the "down" button, he descended to exit into the main lobby.

Walking across the terrazzo floor in the plant-filled atrium, he approached the main entrance doors. He looked through the glass. Helen, in her prim navy suit, stood on the steps out front, holding court. Reporters were frantically taking notes, and snapping pictures. She certainly had matters under control. Whatever she was telling them, they were eating it up. He drew a deep breath, opened a door, and stepped out beside her.

So, this is what the paparazzi were like, he wondered? Pandemonium with cameras.

"Hello," he yelled out, hoping to silence the crowd.

Voices began to mellow and quiet. Eyes glared at him.

He swept the crowd with a narrow-eyed glance.

"I don't know what Helen told you, but understand that my personal life is ... personal. I'd like to keep it that way. Recent news events have been an invasion of privacy, for both me, and Daphne. Helen will be issuing a press release with my statement."

Reporters began to yell out questions.

"Where did you meet?"

"How long have you known each other?"

"Are you engaged?"

He raised his hand.

"Please, I will not be answering questions. How would you like it if I began to interrogate you about your personal life? I'm a private citizen, and this is my headquarters. My employees work here. They have the right not to be intimidated. I came out to address you with the hope that you would kindly leave the premises. Will you please respect my wishes? I'm a reasonable and fair person. Please be fair and reasonable, yourselves. I assure you that Helen will be sending out a statement."

He turned to go back into the building. Helen joined him, as he opened a glass door and walked inside. The rumbling of voices echoed from outside. He glanced back to see the crowd dispersing. They got their photographs, and they would be getting a statement. What else was there? For a moment, he wondered how Meg-Daphne was handling things. The press was surely hounding her, probably more so. Being a famous actress, she was probably used to it, or not. Living life as an anonymous waitress probably allowed her a break from the madness. He began to sympathize.

Thanking Helen for her quick thinking and help, he watched her go back to the elevator. He slunk in an upholstered chair in the middle of the lobby, by a koi pond. There was peace and tranquility in watching fish swim around. Their movement appeared so effortless, and they seemed so calm. He wondered if they ever stressed out.

His private cell rang. He reached in his jeans' pocket, and looked at the ID. Luke.

"Hey," he answered, actually glad to be hearing from his best friend. They hadn't spoken since the shit hit the proverbial fan.

"Hey, you. Just concerned about you. You made international headlines. The press has been patrolling the town. I figured they found you," Luke said.

"Sure did. I addressed them, and they just left. This is crazy, man."

"You really didn't know that Meg was Daphne?"

"Hell, no. I thought she was a struggling waitress. Her normalcy is what attracted me to her. You know how I operate?"

"Yeah, and it usually doesn't work." Luke chuckled.

"How did I know that this average, kind, smart, and old-fashioned woman was Hollywood's bombshell in disguise? She wasn't even blonde."

"I guess she had everyone fooled."

"Seeing her dance at the King Tut was a hint. Figures like hers are not seen often in this town. The way she moved was more than just Kemsit's tutoring."

"Don't beat yourself up." Luke cleared his throat. "So, what's next?"

"What do you mean?"

"You got beat at your own game. All these years, you kept playing blue collar worker around the ladies, hoping that one of them would be okay with it, and accept you for who you are, not what you are. All those stories about women making excuses when they heard your occupation, or saw your beater car. You were beginning to think that all women were after a guy with a pot of gold, not a heart of gold."

"Guilty as charged."

"So, finally one accepted you as a tow motor operator, and didn't object to your ratty jeans, or crummy car."

"I don't wear ratty jeans." River scoffed.

"I beg to differ. Meg didn't object, because she wasn't looking for a guy with money for security. Do you know that she commands $25 million-plus, per movie? And you know what? You are financial equals, so you don't have to worry about having to explain your fortune to her, or be concerned that she's a gold digger. Isn't it actually great that you are equals?"

"Hmm. Sounds good in theory. There are other issues."

"Like what? That she's been voted the sexiest woman on the planet?" Luke chuckled.

"I'm not interested in Daphne. Hell, I've never seen any of her films. Marilyn Monroe stacked blondes just don't interest me. I prefer fresh-scrubbed women, who are wholesome and intelligent ... like Meg."

"Face it. Meg no longer exists."

"Maybe she does?"

Luke sighed. "Meg is Daphne, a superstar. After being outed, Meg can no longer exist. Everyone is now aware of her alter ego, thanks to that pesky reporter."

"I'm a mess. I was in love with a really good actress."

"Maybe she wasn't acting. Maybe Meg was the real woman behind the sex kitten façade."

"Luke, you missed your calling. You should have been a fiction author, not an auto mechanic." He sighed.

"So, what are you going to do?"

"What am I supposed to do?"

"Call her? Go visit her in California?" Luke urged.

"Are you out of your freaking mind?"

"Why?"

"Maybe you need to hear her side of the story?"

"I'm sure that will come out soon enough. I have to come up with a statement about it all, to get the press off my back. I'm sure that she will do the same. End of story."

"My friend, I think that the story is just beginning."

11

Meg was back in her gilded cage, the private compound that she called home, in Hollywood. Behind the iron gate, high brick walls and barbed fences, she was protected from the crowds of paparazzi, reporters, and curiosity seekers. The traditional manor home, with its outbuildings and acreage, was her refuge. She had all of the amenities and luxuries a woman would want. Staff was at her beck and call. Her assistant was working with her publicist and agent in issuing press releases, and filling interview requests. Yet, she had never been more alone.

Her mind drifted to her little apartment above The Classy Chassis. She told her assistant to continue paying the rent, and to pay Estelle to watch over the place. She missed her little private paradise, where she found freedom and contentment. How funny that she had everything she needed at the estate, but not what she wanted.

Would she ever return?

Things would never be the same. No more going back to being Meg, the waitress at the Belle Diner. River, the tow motor operator, was an illusion. That average guy she fell in love with, was not. He was Rutherford Rutledge, a billionaire techno-geek. She couldn't wrap her head around the fact that he was also playing games with his identity. What was his motivation to lie, pretending to be some blue-collar laborer, when he was a technology genius, and one of the wealthiest men in the world? No wonder he found their conversation about Artificial Intelligence interesting, he helped to invent it. Who would have thought that his main headquarters was located just outside of Cairo? Supposedly, he was some nerdy recluse. Yet, she didn't find him to be either.

The photograph of them kissing in the King Tut parking lot was flashed everywhere. You'd think that they had some torrid affair, according to the caption. A first kiss is all that it was. How dare someone invade their privacy to document it? How dare that reporter draw conclusions?

She sighed. The truth had to come out, eventually. Heck, she had discussed her return to the screen with Les before the press descended on her in Cairo. She had also contemplated how to leave the town, and restart her career. Instead of operating on her terms, a reporter made the decision for her. Instead of a discreet excuse, her leaving became an international sensation. As Les said, the publicity was priceless.

Having to leave Meg, and go back to being Daphne was difficult. On one hand, she liked the simplicity of Meg's life. On the other, acting was as natural as breathing. She couldn't have it both ways.

Falling in love with River made her wonder how her life would have been had she quit acting, settled in Cairo, and kept her secret? She had security and money. That was, when River was a tow motor operator, an ordinary guy.

He wasn't. His secret life was exposed. She still couldn't believe that he was also living a lie. Of all the people to meet in a small town in the middle of nowhere.

Thoughts filled her head. Was their meeting an accident, or

did he plan it? Did he know who she was, and target her? Was it one way to get into the life of a Hollywood star? Nerdy techies didn't hang out in her circles. Maybe he and the reporter were in cahoots? He had the money and technology to spy on her. Her heart began to race, and her palms sweat. Could he have had the audacity to pull it off?

"I made an appointment with your hairdresser," Daphne's assistant, Angie, said. "You'll need to go back to short, and platinum blonde for your latest role."

The movie that was scheduled to start filming in a week, was the one that had been delayed during her sabbatical, the one with the $25 million payout. She had promised Les that she'd finish the film, if her next would be the Mata Hari project. He actually contracted one of Hollywood's top scriptwriters for the project, that would be the first under her own production company. Starting her own production company had been on her mind for years. When she told Les, he encouraged it. She needed to diversify. First, she had to finish this film.

"I'm not cutting, or coloring my hair," Daphne replied, lounging on the settee in her spacious, light-filled bedroom.

"But ..." Angie began.

"Find an appropriate wig, one that looks like my old hairstyle. I can wear it in this film Have my stylist play with it. It needs to look natural."

"But, why?"

"I'm growing my hair out for my next role."

"Okay."

"Keep the manicure and pedicure appointments, though. I'm long overdue. Also, schedule me for a facial, and a massage." When in Hollywood, live like a resident of Hollywood.

"By the way, several phone calls have come for you."

Daphne laughed, and rolled her eyes. "Any important calls come to me on my private, Daphne, cell. You know that."

Angie nodded. "I just thought that you might want to speak to this person."

"Why?"

"His name is River Rutledge."

River contacted her? He must have had some pretty good connections to get her home office phone number. That line was reserved strictly for business. This only added credence to her belief that he knew who she was from the beginning.

She drew a finger to her lips.

"No. I don't wish to speak to him. I have nothing to say. Ignore him, and he will go away. If not, block him."

"Are you sure? Really sure?" Angie stared at her, as if she were crazy to avoid him.

"I'm sure. Of course, I'm sure."

Angie shook her head of curls.

"I'm sure," Daphne repeated. She really wasn't.

IMMERSING herself in her latest role, kept her mind off of all that had transpired. Playing a femme fatale moll to a Mafia crime boss wasn't exactly high drama. However, the plot line did offer some pivotal scenes. When she had to reveal herself as a hitman for his rival, things got interesting.

Filming took place on the Amalfi Coast in Italy. The scenery was breathtaking. Medieval villages with narrow cobblestone walks, wrought iron balconies with cascading flowers, and the scent of woodsmoke. Pristine sandy beaches allowed for a swim or two. The fishing villages added color and atmosphere. Steep vertical climbs up stone steps along the coast provided exercise. She half- expected Andre Bocelli to blurt out an aria.

The outdoor scenes were challenging, in the close quarters. Most of the scenes were outdoors, as the inside scenes were to be shot on a soundstage in a studio back lot in Hollywood. The repetition of filming a scene over and over, while the technical crew made adjustments, was exhausting. Filmmaking was a slow and tedious process. Her dressing room was a suite in a nearby *pensione*. The view of the seaport from her balcony was breathtaking. She observed the fishing boats depart, and return with their catches. She spent a great deal of time seated, waiting to be called for her next scene, or a repeat of the last. At least it was superior to waiting in a trailer on the studio lot.

She thought back to the time when she was young, naïve Meg, just starting out in the business. Waitressing during the day, acting classes at night, and fitting in auditions when she could. Occasionally, she landed a role in a play at a small theater. One of those leading roles put her on the radar.

"Miss Miller," the director said, approaching her, as she walked to the dank dressing room after a performance. "Someone wants to meet you."

Rolling her eyes, she answered, "Not another one."

"This is different. It's Les Porter, from the Porter Agency in Hollywood."

She spun around to face him. "*The* Les Porter?"

"One and the same. He's waiting in the Green Room.

"Okay."

The director smiled, and winked. "Break a leg."

Hollywood's top talent agent wanted to speak to her? This was interesting. Before meeting him, she popped in the dressing room to fluff her hair and touch up her makeup. Still wearing her slit-up-to-there, form-fitting costume, from her stage role as a sexy harlot, she sashayed into the Green Room, a lounge-waiting room.

"Miss Miller." The tall, distinguished man with salt and pepper hair, and dark eyes stood to greet her.

"Mr. Porter."

She approached, shook his hand, and he pointed to a chair for her to sit. They sat.

"Your acting and stage presence are quite impressive. Honestly, I haven't seen anyone with your natural charisma in years."

She swallowed hard. She sensed that this was more than a complement. "Thank you."

"No, thank *you*." He leaned forward. "I've seen this play three nights in a row, just to observe you. Never since Marilyn Monroe, has a woman enchanted an audience with her innocent sexuality. It's a trait missing in modern Hollywood. You have the face, and the figure that would light up a screen. I'd like you to come to Universal Studios for a screen test. There's a new film auditioning actresses for the lead. It's a slapstick comedy, featuring a not-so-dumb blonde."

"But, I'm not blonde." Her hair was its natural mousy brown.

"That can easily be changed."

"I ... I'm flattered and overwhelmed." She was.

"Here, take my card. Think it over. Let me know, tomorrow, and I can make arrangements." He handed her a business card.

Little did she know that this would be the beginning of her career, and her life. That first film took her to Rome, Italy.

A knock rattled her door. Angie called from the hallway.

"Come in," Daphne said.

"Hey."

"They want me on set?" Daphne asked.

"Not yet. You got a phone call."

"I didn't hear my cell ring."

"He called the set."

"Who?"

"River Rutledge."

"Now, he is following me around the world? Calling me here?"

"You have to hand it to him. He's persistent."

"Angie, I told you to block him, and disregard his calls."

"I just thought ... maybe ..."

Daphne shook her head. "No. Just no."

Angie left, and she drew a deep breath. Her heart and her mind were at odds. In her heart, she loved the handsome, intelligent, and quirky River. Yet, her mind couldn't forgive him for his deception, and being Rutherford, whatever kind of name that was. He got his publicity for kissing the famous Daphne. Couldn't he just get over it, and move on? Tears pooled in her eyes. She couldn't get over it. What she felt for him was real.

12

Daphne wouldn't answer or return his telephone calls. River had exhausted all of his resources and contacts. Getting the private cell number of Daphne was impossible, even for a tech insider. He called her office, her agent, her publicist, and even the set of her latest film, in Italy. He was certain that someone told her of his calls. Apparently, she wasn't interested in talking to him.

Why was she angry at him? He was as much a victim of the reporter's story as she. Both of them were guilty of deception. He meant no harm, by just protecting himself. Before their relationship progressed, he was going to come clean. What was her game? Why would Hollywood's "It" girl land in middle-of-nowhere Cairo? Why would she go through the trouble of dressing down? Why would she waitress? Why would she choose him to date? Was it in preparation for a future film role? Was he just another prop, to get her into character? He wanted answers, but couldn't speak to her. She was evading him.

When his tech friend, Sanjay, called from Los Angeles, River had an idea. Sanjay owned a very successful software firm, and was well-connected. He thrived on socializing with the rich and famous. A film buff, living near Hollywood, he was a fixture at movie premieres, parties, and award shows. He even produced an award-winning film short, and a documentary lauded at Sundance.

"By chance, do you know Daphne?" River asked.

Sanjay chuckled. "I think that you know her better than me, my friend."

"I knew her alias, Meg. I'd like to meet Daphne, to ask her a few questions."

"Is she now playing hard to get?"

"She's not communicating."

"Doesn't bode well for your relationship."

"Whatever it was."

Sanjay chuckled again. "Tell you what? You are in luck."

"How?" His mood lightened.

"I have an invitation to the wrap party for her latest film, 'Mob Boss.' I can bring a guest. That guest could be you. That is, if you can get out here by Friday night."

It was Wednesday.

"I can make it happen." He could call his pilot, and get a corporate jet ready.

"Good. Meet me at my place by Six. The party is at Seven at the producer's Malibu beach house."

"You're on."

He would call his assistant to arrange transportation, and make hotel reservations. River was going Hollywood.

THE SPRAWLING CREAM stucco home with the red tile roof was stunning. A monolith, perched above the sandy beach, it loomed over the ocean. A wall of windows faced a spacious wood deck. An infinity pool and spa were on one end. An outdoor kitchen on the other. Palm trees added shade and ambiance. Groups of people were gathered in animated conversation. Drinks in hand, their voices created a jumble, drowning out the Reggae band at the other end.

River stepped on to the deck with Sanjay. With his coiled turban and Madras tunic, Sanjay stood out in the crowd of preppy sportcoats and glamorous sundresses. The women were at least half the age of the men, River observed. Most were augmented and enhanced, resembling Barbie more than natural women. He found the scene disconcerting.

A man with silver hair, a broad smile, and a neatly tied Ascot, approached. "Sanjay, welcome. One day, we will be celebrating your feature film."

"Maybe one day. One small step at a time," Sanjay said. "May I introduce my friend, Rutherford Rutledge."

"The tech genius." The man reached out to shake his hand. "I'm Paul Torres, producer of this film."

"You can call me, River," he said.

"Let me introduce you around."

Paul led them to a group of chatting couples. From the corner of his eye, River saw her. How could he not notice the statuesque blonde in towering sandals, and figure-enhancing leopard print halter dress? The fluffy, short platinum hair was a departure from Meg's brown tresses. She was chatting with two couples, talking with her hands, moving like a dancer. So, this was Daphne?

Small talk with strangers bored him to death, but he tried to be friendly. River was reminded why he disliked the superficial party scene. He took a few sips of wine, and set down his glass.

"You know the star?" Paul asked, taking River by the arm, toward Daphne.

She turned, and they locked eyes. Her gaze was wide. Her face seemed a lighter shade of pale. Unlike the Meg he knew, she was made up like a star. Her eyes were lined, with sparkling shadow and long, false lashes. Her cheekbones were highlighted to accent their depth. Lipstick and gloss gave her lips a pouting expression. The hair framed her face like cotton candy.

"Hello," she greeted in soft purr. Even her voice was different. Only the blue of her eyes remained unchanged.

He took her hand, and an electric pulse startled him.

"Hi, Meg ... Daphne," he said.

"Come, Sanjay." Paul winked, leading Sanjay by the arm, toward other guests.

"What are you doing here?" Daphne asked, in a voice more aligned with Meg.

"I was invited. Sanjay is a friend from my Silicon Valley days."

"To the wrap party for my film? Isn't this a little too coincidental?" She glared at him.

He shrugged.

"Why are you after me? All of these phone calls, and now, this?"

"I wanted to talk to you."

"The tabloid told me all I needed to know."

Guests were beginning to congregate closer.

"It didn't tell the whole story."

"Of how you deceived me?" She waved her hands. "We can't discuss this here. I don't need an audience. Let's go down to the beach."

He followed her, walking across the crowded deck, past the band, and down the winding wood stairway to the private beach. The pristine sand and crashing waves were a departure from the noisy party above. The breeze was clean and crisp.

One step in the sand, and Daphne's heels sunk in. She bent down to remove her shoes. River steadied her. After, she tossed the shoes on the steps.

"Why not?' He stepped out of his loafers, and did the same.

She shook her head, and touched her hair. "I still can't believe that you're here?"

"Hey, your film sounds like a winner."

They walked barefoot in the sand, along the shoreline, away from the house and party.

She turned to face him, hands on her hips. "Okay, fess up. You knew who I was all along, yet played the game to meet me. Why?"

"What are you talking about? I met Meg, and had no idea she was Daphne."

"Yeah, right."

"I had no interest in Daphne. If I had, Sanjay could have introduced us long ago."

"Why did you lie? Tow motor operator!"

He told her about his *modus operandi* in meeting women.

"So, I wanted a woman who would love me for who I was, not what I was," he summed up.

"When were you going to tell me?"

"Soon, when I knew that our love was real."

"Our love? Ha!" She continued to walk, hips swaying.

"So, tell me, what was your game? Studying for a role? Being an actress?"

She spun around. "How dare you."

"What was I to think? Especially, when the article came out."

"I thought that you tipped off the reporter."

"I stay out of the spotlight, and live under the radar. You don't. The publicity probably did you good."

"I didn't ask for it."

"If not for the article, would you have ever told me who you were, or would you have just disappeared?" River asked with a scowl.

"I would have told you, eventually."

"Who was this Meg?"

"Meg is me."

"Ha!" He scoffed.

She sat on a piece of driftwood, and stared at the water. "I am Meg. Margaret Miller."

He sat next to her, and she didn't move.

"Daphne is my stage name, and my alias. She's the opposite of the real me. I am the Meg you met in Cairo." She slid her hand down her body. "This is a Hollywood fantasy. I was escaping that fantasy. You have no idea how difficult it is keeping up her façade. I've spent ten years being Daphne. I went on a sabbatical to go find myself. The press found me."

Tears glistened in her eyes, and she choked on the words. He wanted to believe her. A lump formed in his throat.

"Did you find yourself?" he asked.

"I'd like to think that I did." She glanced up at him. "The time away offered reflection and introspection. I went back to my roots, living like a starving artist waiting tables. I had to go back to the past, to plan my future."

"Have you planned your future?"

She nodded, clearing her throat. "My career is headed in a new direction. It's going to be good."

He was happy for her, yet sad for himself. Where did he fit in? Did he fit in?

"I think that you'll be surprised," she said, with a smile.

"Nothing will surprise me anymore."

"We'd better be heading back." She stood, smoothing her dress.

"I'm sure the party misses its star."

"I'm only as good as my last film. It's an unending cycle."

"I understand. I'm only as good as my latest patent."

"You know, You're really not nerdy."

He chuckled.

"Well, I better transform into Daphne. You know, the walk, the gestures, and the voice." She sighed.

"I prefer Meg."

"I do, too."

13

Daphne began to think that she was destined to portray the exotic Mata Hari. Mata's real name, Margaretha, was similar to her name, Margaret. Both had an alias. She was Daphne, named after a Greek water nymph. Margaretha was Mata Hari, "Eye of the Dawn." Both were rather mysterious, and liked to perform. They were both of Dutch ethnicity. However, Meg's life was about as boring, as Mata's was adventurous. Both overcame adversity, though, she didn't have a violent husband, lose her children, have a string of lovers, a sordid past, or have to face death by firing squad as a spy. Portraying such an intriguing woman was exciting. Finally, she had a role with depth, history, and the variety that could showcase her many talents, including dance. Though she didn't resemble Mata, she could capture her essence; her heart and soul.

Lounging on the down-filled sofa in her spacious living room, wrapped in a chenille bathrobe. She sipped tea, while reading the script. She inhaled the comforting aroma of lemon and mint. The house was quiet, the way she liked it. The staff were gone for the evening. Only security remained, at their separate quarters. A gentle rain was tapping at the windows.

She closed her eyes, envisioning herself as young Mata, making her Paris debut in 1905. Using Egypt and Asia as her influence, she danced in a provocative and flirtatious way, shedding her veils until revealing a jeweled metal breastplate and hip belt, over a nude body stocking. As a renowned entertainer, she elevated the art of exotic dance as respectable in polite society.

Looking at the grandfather's clock in a corner, she noted it being only seven o'clock, ten o'clock New York Time. Kemsit would be ending her last class. She wondered if her teacher would like a respite from Cairo, to come to Hollywood. She needed a choreographer to capture the essence of Mata Hari for the big screen.

A LIMOUSINE WAS SENT to LAX, and Kemsit was brought to Daphne's Hollywood compound. Daphne welcomed her on the steps of her mansion, under the veranda flanked by soaring Corinthian columns. Giddy, like a school girl, seeing Kemsit emerge from the sleek, black automobile, she clapped and jumped up and down. The mode of transportation suited Kemsit. With her shimmering black hair, sleek figure encased in tight jeans and bell-sleeved top, she looked like the Hollywood star. Daphne ran down the steps to embrace her in greeting.

"I'm so glad that you were able to come," Daphne gushed.

"It's not every day I'm invited to Hollywood." Kemsit glanced at the surroundings. "This is a far cry from the apartment in Cairo, no?"

Daphne pulled away, and shrugged. "This is a house. The apartment was a home."

Kemsit met her gaze.

"Come in. I'll show you around. Your bags will be brought to your room," Daphne explained, taking her arm, and leading her into the house.

Kemsit was her first house guest. Never having had time to entertain, this visit was special. She looked forward to the reunion with a friend, and dancing again. There was a perk in producing your own film. She also had the freedom to hire her own crew. Everyone operated on her schedule. She was grateful that Kemsit agreed to be her film's dance choreographer.

They entered the marble foyer, with its double circular staircases, and domed stained glass ceiling. Ornate scrolled ironwork banisters accented the wide marble stairs, with red oriental runners. A layered crystal chandelier hung above a circular crystal table, with a vase overflowing with red roses.

"This is so beautiful," Kemsit said, twirling around in the cavernous space.

"I have an image to uphold."

"Hollywood's queen, in her palace."

Or gilded cage, Daphne thought.

"Follow me," Daphne said, walking toward an arched doorway. "We will start in the east wing."

Daphne proceeded to give Kemsit a tour of her sprawling home. There was the posh living room, with its stunning antiques, that Daphne had collected during her travels around the world, and the elegant dining room with its long burled-wood banquet table, buffet and china cabinet. Each room had a fireplace. On the fireplace mantels were perched her awards, Golden Globes, and Academy Awards. The commercial kitchen was shimmering stainless and granite, with a stocked, walk-in pantry, and butler's pantry. A glass solarium served as the breakfast room. A multi-tiered deck ran the length of the back of the house, with access from the solarium, living room, and upstair's bedrooms. It overlooked a tropically landscaped backyard with infinity pool and spa, with a pool house beyond.

"The west wing has the library, offices for my staff, and my office," Daphne explained.

"Is it oval?" Kemsit chuckled.

"Not quite."

Daphne showed her bathrooms that were bigger than the living room in her Cairo apartment. Upstairs were guest bedrooms and baths, one designated for Kemsit. Daphne's master suite was her favorite room. Her canopied king-sized bed was set on a platform, velvet drapes tied with tassel cords at each post. Matching drapes were drawn back from the floor-length windows. A monitor took up a far wall. Built-in cabinets, and a counter with a refrigerator, microwave, and beverage service were on another. A chaise, tables, sofa and loveseat flanked a marble fireplace.

Daphne opened a door, and they entered a wide hall. On one side was a glamour bath, complete with sunken marble tub and glassed-in shower. On the other was a walk-in closet, lit by crystal chandeliers. Built-in cabinets, racks and drawers were filled with designer clothes, shoes, purses, and accessories.

"Image is everything," Daphne said, with a sigh.

They took an elevator down to the walk-out basement. Exiting into a recreation room, Daphne pointed out the "night-club," with its stocked bar, bistro tables and chairs, DJ booth and stage, and wood dance floor with a shimmering disco ball overhead. In one corner was a dancer's pole.

"Don't ask." Daphne laughed.

Doors led to the outdoor stone patio with outdoor kitchen, living room, fireplace, with the pool area beyond.

"Must be fun for entertaining," Kemsit commented.

"There have been some wild parties here. All business." Daphne shrugged. "Now, the fun place."

Daphne slid open doors, and they entered a theater,

complete with vintage velvet theater seats, a theater-sized screen, and a concession stand with popcorn popper and beverage service.

"This is where I preview daily cuts, unedited versions of my films, and films before they are premiered and released to the public. I also love to watch classic films. I'll take Cary Grant and Clark Gable over any modern Hollywood hunk."

Going across the "nightclub," Daphne slid open a set of doors to reveal a fully-equipped gym, treadmills and stair-steppers facing a wall of windows with a view of the woods and Hollywood hills. Opening another door, they entered a dance studio. Wireless speakers were set in the ceiling, and two parallel walls were mirrored.

"The floor is sprung wood," Daphne explained. "The sound system is built-in."

"Impressive."

"This is where we can work on choreography, and practice. I hope it suits you?"

"It's perfect."

"Great." Daphne smiled, and opened another door. "This is the costume room. I have some samples for Mata Hari. I'd like to make sure they are dance-worthy, before they are finished."

"Kemsit grinned. "They will be, when we are done."

"I don't want you to feel trapped here. My intention is not to work you 24/7, or take up every waking moment. I want you to make yourself at home. If you want to sightsee, I can arrange a driver and a car."

"Thank you."

Daphne glanced at her smartwatch. "Dinner is probably ready, and I bet you're starving."

THE NEXT MORNING, after a light breakfast, Daphne presented the movie script to Kemsit, highlighting the dance scenes. She also gave her a recording of the musical score, especially the dance sequences.

"If the music isn't right, the composer can make adjustments," Daphne said. "I want you to become familiar with the story."

"This is fabulous. May I sit by the pool to review these?" Kemsit asked.

"Of course, go anywhere you wish. While you are here, this is your home. If you need anything, staff will assist. From coffee to lunch, from pen to paper, anything, they will help."

"You are spoiling me. You already paid my transportation, am providing room and board, paying me a fee, and giving me onscreen credit. You are very generous."

"I like to share my success. I can't think of someone more worthy."

"You are too kind, Meg ... Daphne."

"I answer to either. Well, I have to go to the studio. The film is in its preliminary stages. Scouts are traveling, finding set locations. Set designers are planning, and constructing sets. Casting is still taking place, with screen tests booked. So many details. I will be back, later. Perhaps, we can discuss the script and music after dinner?"

"Sounds like a plan."

AFTER DINNER, Daphne and Kemsit changed into dance leggings, midriff tops, and coin belts. They went to the downstairs' studio. Daphne put the movie's musical score on the sound system.

"To get us in the mood," Daphne said.

"The influence is highly Egyptian, with an Asian, and Indian influence," Kemsit said. "Mata Hari spent her childhood in Java, where she learned the native dances. She was an original classic cabaret dancer, though, who melded the different cultures into her own flamboyant style. She unveiled to reveal her body," Kemsit explained.

"Imagine, dancing in a nude body stocking with a skimpy bra, belt and skirt, in 1905, during the Belle Epoque?"

"Very provocative."

"Reminds me of Debra Paget performing that snake dance in 'The Indian Tomb,' in 1959," Daphne said.

"She left little to the imagination. Yet, it was sensual, not sexual. Your dance will be sensual, as well."

"My dance needs to reveal why Mata was accepted to dance at private parties, and some of Europe's greatest theaters," Daphne said.

"She was exotic, and her dance evoked a mysterious culture. Though her dance wasn't 100% authentic, her audience didn't know. They bought into the forbidden. It's why belly dance is popular."

"This movie will, hopefully, make it more popular."

"We can hope." Kemsit winked. "Let's do some stretches and warm-up exercises. We will go over some dance moves that may be candidates for your dance. Though I am Egyptian, I have studied dance from other cultures. We can add some Asian and Indian moves."

"It's too bad there isn't a film of Mata Hari dancing." Daphne sighed.

"I think it is good that there isn't. You can make this dance your own. No need to copy. As you have probably determined, I am not into copycat dancers. To me each dancer is unique, and should have her own style. My pet peeve are dancers who choreograph other dancers, down to facial expression. I also don't want to see a student be a mini-me of her instructor. It's why I urge my students to attend dance seminars, workshops, and classes with other instructors, and to watch video instruction. Each dancer must create her own style."

"So, I will be dancing my own version of Mata Hari?"

Kemsit nodded. "You will not be Greta Garbo or the lovely Russian girl in the series. We will collaborate to make your dance uniquely your own. The goal is to make it unforgettable."

"I'm so glad that I landed in Cairo, and met you."

"It was destiny. I believe that everything happens for a reason."

14

D aphne checked her cell phone. River had called again. She had given him her personal cell number after the party, at a weak moment. He had returned to Cairo the next morning, and had called her several times. Always at the wrong time. She was either in a production meeting, practicing with Kemsit, working out in her gym, or just not in the mood for chatter. She was going over the film script for the umpteenth time, seated by the pool, when he rang.

"Hello," she answered in her kittenish Daphne voice.

"Meg?"

She sighed, returning to her normal voice, "Yes, River."

"You are not an easy lady to get a hold of."

"I'm working on a film, and have little free time."

"You are always working."

"I don't have a choice. Keeping a Hollywood career going is 24/7."

"How's your big project?" he asked.

"One step at a time. It's coming together."

"You're the talk of Cairo,"

"Still?"

"You've stolen the town's infamous belly dance instructor."

"Only temporarily. Charise and Emily have been taking on her classes and dance companies. Kemsit's been in touch. You know, she's a bit of a control freak, when it comes to the studio."

"How's it going?" he asked.

"Kemsit is incredible. You'd think that she's been reincarnated from Ancient Egypt. The dance she's choreographing with me is mesmerizing. I feel possessed, like in a trance when I perform it."

"Do I get a sneak preview?" He chuckled.

"No one does. You'll have to see the movie in the theater, like everyone else."

"Damn. When can I see you?"

She paused, thinking. Her schedule left little free time. After chatting with him at the party, she did want to see him again. He was one of the few people with whom she could be herself. Oddly enough, she missed him. A silly idea, that could actually work, crossed her mind.

"Well?" he asked.

"Would you like to attend the premiere of '*Mob Boss*?' You could ride with me, and be my escort. Understand, that the press will be merciless, and we will be linked romantically in all the tabloids."

"Again?" He chuckled.

"On second thought, maybe it isn't such a great idea."

"Maybe, this techno nerd needs to start living dangerously."

"Here's your opportunity."

"Hmm."

"Kemsit will be attending."

"Sanjay will be jealous."

"I can send him a ticket."

"This is so crazy."

"This will be fun. I need some fun, so I've rented a villa for me, my staff, and my ticketed guests, for the weekend."

"Wait. A villa?"

"In the port city of Salerno, where the premiere is being held."

"Salerno?"

"On the Amalfi Coast, in south-western Italy."

"Italy?"

"The movie was filmed on the Amalfi Coast."

"When?"

"September 3."

"I'll have to clear my schedule, and inform my pilot."

WAS he out of his freaking mind? Flying to Italy for the weekend to escort the world's most famous sex symbol to her movie premiere? River was not into a jet-setting lifestyle. He was a homebody, whose life revolved around his job. An anonymous loner, he preferred to stay in the background. Avoiding the spotlight, publicity, and media had been a way of life. He could live in peace and quiet. Only Luke knew who he was, in Cairo. To everyone else, he was just another low-key, blue-jean-wearing, blue collar guy. No one connected him to the R&R of his international corporation. He had preferred to live a "normal" life in public.

The tabloid story, linking he and Daphne changed everything. No longer could he stroll into the Belle Diner for a quiet, leisurely breakfast. Dinner at The Coffee Cup Bistro, now put him at the head of the line, with stares and whispers. The tow motor line, and beater automobile no longer offered cover. Women were coming on to him with regularity. He didn't ask for, or want the attention.

Often, he would wake up in the morning thinking that nothing had changed. Somehow, it just been a bad dream. Yet, when he left his house, he was reminded. River was Rutherford

Rutledge, technology czar, and billionaire, a man who changed the world. There were Gates, Jobs, Musk, and Rutledge.

Unlike the others, he was linked to the hottest actress on the planet. Yet, he didn't view her as such. To him, she was still Meg, just plain Meg. He wondered if he could ever accept her as Daphne.

SALERNO WAS POSTCARD-WORTHY, its harbor bustling with commercial and pleasure vessels. Hillside villas and businesses with red-tiled roofs, towered over historic town center, with the ornate bell tower of the Duomo, Salerno Cathedral. River was reminded, that with all of his wealth, he hadn't traveled much. He was all work, all the time. Taking a weekend off was unheard of. Even his pilot was stunned, when he informed him of his plans. Instead of his small jet, the Gulfstream had to be prepped, and staff assigned for the overseas journey. A lot of schedule shuffling and preparation were necessary for the weekend. Peering out of the window of the limousine, the scenery was breathtaking enough to make it worth it. Daphne had sent the limousine to greet him at the Capodichino International Airport, in Naples, for the thirty-five-minute ride to Salerno.

The villa perched on the hillside looked straight out of Hollywood. The towering pink stucco clad building had terraces overlooking the town and water. Climbing vines and overflowing flower boxes added color. Potted trees and plants added additional ambiance, lining the cobblestone walk leading to the villa's entrance. The chauffeur opened the door, and River inhaled the fresh air from the Gulf of Salerno.

"They are expecting you, Sir. I will have your bags delivered to your suite," the chauffeur said, in a smooth Italian accent.

"Thank you." He gazed up at the imposing villa. So, this is how the Hollywood elite traveled?

He stopped at the massive carved front door, and it squeaked open. Daphne appeared, with a broad smile on her made-up face. She raked a hand through her fluffy platinum hair, a color he had a hard time adapting to. He preferred the natural Meg.

"I knew it was you," she squealed, embracing him, and kissing him on the cheek. The gesture warmed his heart, and other places. She generated an electrical energy that he found baffling.

She was poured into skin-tight jeans and a black 'Mob Boss' tee shirt. He noticed that she was barefoot. Stepping back, she placed her hand on her hips. "Come on in. We were just getting ready for lunch."

"I guess I had good timing."

"How was your flight?" She waved him inside.

"Perfect. I haven't flown overseas for years, ever since I moved manufacturing from China, back to the U.S."

He scanned the spacious foyer, with its ornately carved and gilded columns, winding marble staircase with iron banisters leading to a mezzanine. The terrazzo floor was inlaid with seashells and flecks of gold. Red roses filled vases on the side tables, reflecting on gilded mirrors. A breeze blew through from a bank of open French doors out back. The scent was of sea and salt.

"Everyone's out back, on the terrace," she said, leading him toward the open doors.

"This is quite a place."

"My assistant, Angie, is really good at making arrangements. She found this fabulous rental."

Swanky, by his standards, he realized that he had the funds to purchase such a place, if he desired. For some odd reason, he hadn't had the inclination to buy much. He invested in his business, not in himself. The jets and Gulfstream were corporate. His farm was his only real estate holding, save for corporate offices and plants. His wardrobe was minimal, consisting of jeans and shirts, a couple business suits and a tux, for business. His attire for the day were khaki slacks and a blue and white striped Oxford shirt, with the sleeves rolled up. He was conservative, by Hollywood standards. Daphne's lifestyle lent him pause.

He followed her out on the terrace, with its marble statues, potted herbs, and flowers. The view was breathtaking. The turquoise water of the bay shimmered in the sunlight. Sailboats and yachts bobbed in the water, while commercial vessels skimmed the surface. Lush hillsides with colorful structures built into the hills surrounded them in beauty.

"Great view, isn't it?" she said. "The Tyrrhenian Sea on the beautiful Gulf of Salerno."

"Incredible."

"I think that you will recognize some of these people," she said, as they approached a long wood table, set with woven placemats, ceramic-ware, hand-blown glasses, and tableware.

He smiled. Familiar faces smiled back, and rose to greet him.

"Hey, Sanjay," he said. His friend with the Madras tunic and turban seemed to fit right in.

They shook hands.

"Thank you for getting me invited," Sanjay said.

Kemsit reached out her hand. "How are things back in Cairo?"

"Nothing changes," he said.

"You remember Paul Torres, the producer of this film? Paul's joining us for lunch." Daphne smiled at the distinguished, gray-haired man.

The men shook hands.

"Yes, at the wrap party. I guess this is the big event," River said.

"Make or break time, though I do think the critics will be raving about Daphne's performance," Paul said.

A dark-haired younger man, added, "Oscar material."

"Thanks, Greg. Greg Popovich, the film's director," Daphne said. "Also joining us for lunch."

"I'm sorry that my co-star, Riccardo Mandolini, is arriving later," Daphne added. "You can meet him at the party after tomorrow's premiere."

"Okay."

"And, Angie, my assistant," Daphne introduced.

The studious-looking curly haired brunette fit the job description, with her tortoise-shell glasses, and prim linen business suit.

"Nice meeting you."

"Please, sit down, and make yourself at home," Daphne said.

Right, make himself at home? Who was she kidding, River thought? Having never seen any of Daphne's films, or any films, or television in years, he was a fish out of water. Maybe it was a good thing. The group of Hollywood insiders did not impress or intimidate him. His friend, Sanjay, was gloating, as he sat, fanning his cloth napkin on his lap.

Lunch was very ... Italian. Caprese salad, fresh fish, eggplant parmesan, spaghetti, Neopolitan pizza, red wine, and fizzing water with lemon, were served. Gelato and hazelnuts were offered for dessert, with cappuccino.

"The best restaurant in Salerno, Ristorante Cicirinella, catered this delightful meal," Daphne said. "We all have free time until tomorrow's big event. The town is made for exploring. There is a scenic promenade for walks. If you are so inclined, there is a pool and spa here, or you can go down to the sandy beach. Dinner here is served at eight, unless you decide to dine in town. Your choice. Enjoy."

River surveyed the infinity pool overlooking the harbor, and hot tub. Decisions, decisions. He wasn't used to having free time.

Sanjay rose, setting down his napkin. "Kemsit, are you game for a walk through the scenic Old Town?"

She stood. "Why not?"

Winking at Daphne, she left with him.

"Interesting," River muttered.

"Why?" Daphne asked. "What's wrong with a little fun?"

"I'm hitting the Duomo," Paul said. "My son's name is Matthew. He'd be impressed that I visited the church, which bears his name, and where Saint Matthew is buried." He rose to leave. "Thank you for the exquisite lunch, and company, Daphne. I will see you later."

"*Ciao*, Paul." She blew him a kiss.

Greg stood. "I'll see you all later. I need to decompress at my hotel."

He left.

Angie stood. "I will finalize all plans for tomorrow night. Your agent, Les, is arriving in the morning. Your publicist, stylist, hairdresser and makeup artist are arriving at five. Your stylist will have your gown and accessories ready. The jeweler is arriving at six. In the morning, you can try on everything, in case there is a need for alterations."

"Thank you," Daphne said, as Angie left.

"I guess it leaves you and me," River said, meeting Daphne's gaze.

She let out a sigh, and sat back. "This is hard work."

He shrugged. "Looks like fun to me."

"You have no idea."

"Well, do you have any plans for the rest of the day, and tonight?"

"Yes."

His expression changed from hopeful, to disappointed. His grin turned into a frown.

She laughed. "My plan is to put on some shorts and a tunic, remove this wig and makeup, and stroll into town with you, incognito."

His smile returned. "Wig?"

"I'm letting my hair grow out for '*Mata Hari*', but I still have to look like my character in '*Mob Boss,*' for movie promotion."

"So, I get to be with Meg this afternoon?"

"Yes. Absolutely. No one will recognize me, here, and I can relax."

"Sounds like a good plan." He liked her plan, a lot.

BEING with Meg was like going back in time, to their days in Cairo. No bombshell looks and kittenish voice. After she changed, they proceeded to go for a walk. No one paid attention to her as Meg, and he liked it.

"Angie recommended some sites, and downloaded some historical information, and a map on my phone," Daphne said.

"That's great."

"Hmm, Salerno was home to the world's first medical school," Daphne read. "The town was a center for art, culture, and education in the 16th century. Sadly, it suffered from earthquakes, plagues, and foreign invasion."

He took her hand, as they proceeded to walk down to the *Lungomare Trieste,* the city's famous promenade, lined with towering palm trees

"Translated, it means, 'along the sea,'" Daphne read. "Sort of resembles the French Riviera, another great location for film premieres."

They descended stone steps into the historic Medieval core of the city, starting at the *Piazza della Libertia.* Narrow streets

and alleyways, surrounded by towering stone buildings lined
the maze of streets, with boutiques and shops. Iron balconies of
upstairs' residences dripped with ivy and flowers. Painted
merchant signs waved overhead, like flags beckoning one to
enter. Like stepping back in time, merchant and artisan workshops dotted the stone walkways. Alleys were filled with liquor
shops, clothing and leather shops, ceramic stores, shops selling
candles, homemade pasta, olive oil, and chocolate. The breeze
was scented with each as they passed.

"The temptation is real," Daphne said.

"Why not give in, and go inside?"

"No," she said. "The last thing I need, are more things. I
did enough damage during my free time, while filming the
movie."

He laughed. "Tell you what, I'm going into that liquor store
to buy some limoncello, that I'm hoping you will share
with me."

"Now, that sounds like a good idea."

He went in, and emerged with a bottle in a paper bag.

"You look like the typical American wino."

"Someone has to be the ugly American." He winked.

"We will find a special place to imbibe," she said.

They walked down to the beach. The sand was dotted with
orange, green and blue parasols and beach chairs, sun worship-
pers hidden beneath them. The water was liquid turquoise. At
the nearby port, fishing boats were returning with their catches.
The pungent scent of fish and sea filled the air. They walked
out on the dock, observing buckets of squirming fish. Looking
back to shore, the rainbow-hued buildings lining the shore
added quaintness. The arched stone Medieval aquaduct added
history.

They strolled toward the Maritime Station and the *Molo
Manfredi Porto di-Salerno*, along a stretch of pier. Finding a
concrete bench overlooking the sea, with the cityscape of

Salerno and mountain range behind them, they sat. River removed the bottle and two plastic cups from the bag.

"Good. I thought we were going to share the bottle," she said.

"I'm not that ugly." He laughed.

Daphne held the cups, while he poured.

She handed a cup to River, and they tapped cups.

"To an adventurous weekend," he said.

"*Salut.*"

They sipped.

"That is really smooth," Daphne said.

"Remember, it's mostly straight vodka, with just a little sugar syrup, and a lot of lemon. It packs quite a punch," River explained.

"Perfect," she said, and turning to meet his gaze. "How do you know so much about making this stuff?"

He chuckled. "My mom loves to infuse things in vodka. She makes her own vanilla extract, and is a master at martini's."

"Where does your mom live?"

"My parents retired to a condo in Naples, Florida." He smiled, thinking of his last visit, and how he was overdue for another.

"That's wonderful."

"You never said anything about your family."

She sipped her drink. "There's not much to say. My mother was an unwed junkie, and I grew up on the streets. I've been on my own, as long as I can remember. I'm sure she doesn't even know I'm alive."

"I'd like to hear your story."

"I've never told it to anyone."

"Your secrets are safe with me."

She drew a deep breath and told him her story of running away from a drug-infested apartment, after an attempted rape by one of her mother's many paramours. Hers was a story of struggle and perseverance, mixed in with hard work, and a little luck.

Looking at the dullness in her eyes, there was profound sadness. "The world's most famous actress is, essentially, an orphan?"

She nodded, tears glistening. "All of this fame and fortune, and no one to share it with."

"One day, you will meet the right person, get married, and create your own family. You won't be alone, and they will share in your success," he said. The thought had a lump form in his throat.

"You think?" She swept a tear from her eye.

"I do, because I feel the same."

The way she stared at him, made him warm and fuzzy inside. Was she the "right person?"

"We should head back. Let's stop at the Duomo, first." She stood.

"I'm game."

"I HAVE AN AFFINITY FOR HISTORIC CHURCHES," Daphne admitted, as they stood before the 12th Century, Cathedral of San Matteo, Saint Matthew.

"My parents are avid churchgoers. Me? Not so much. I guess it's the engineer-scientist in me." He shrugged.

"I find serenity in the architecture, the stained glass, and the organ music. When I travel, I make a point of visiting the important churches and cathedrals."

"In Italy, there are so many, visiting them can be a full-time job."

"Agree." She looked at her phone, clicking on the guide. "This cathedral is a symbol of the Italian Renaissance. Do you know that Pope Gregory VII is buried here? It is said that Saint Matthew is, as well."

"Consecrated ground?"

"It is a church." She looked up at the grand white edifice, of travertine marble and brick with triangular pediment, and delicate arched porticos sprawled on three sides. As they stood in the front courtyard, she contemplated the entrance.

"If not for the religious symbolism, it resembles a villa, more than a church," River commented.

"Right, with a bell tower." She pointed to the structure that towered over the city, with its small arcades, mullioned windows, and bells. "It's Norman-Arabic in style."

"Let's go inside," he said.

Daphne noted the two marble lions flanking the Byzantine-style bronze doors, with their figured panels and crosses, telling the story of Jesus' life.

"This quite a multi-cultural structure."

"I love the uniqueness of churches and cathedrals. The architecture is fascinating, the craftsmanship incredible."

They entered, stepping into the portico. Arched columns towered over ancient Roman sarcophagi. A grand central apse, and two smaller apses were featured. Facing the interior nave, two elevated platforms to celebrate the liturgy were covered in blue, red and gold Arabic-Sicilian mosaics. Two aisles were divided by towering arches. Ceiling frescoes depicted the gospel of Matthew, and a history of Salerno.

Daphne made a sign of the cross, and mouthed a prayer. Though not overtly religious, she was spiritual. Her prayer was one she recited often, thanking God for her success, and hoping that she could make a difference in the world.

"Making a wish?" he asked.

"Sort of."

"For a moment there, you appeared as pensive as Mother Teresa."

"I try to follow her example, by helping others."

"I try to make a difference, too. My charity, The R&R Foundation donates to the science departments at high schools and universities, award scholarships, and internships. I also host and finance a computer and technology camp for underprivileged children. I fly them out to my farm, to spend a week studying, experimenting, and exploring. They also do fun things, like hiking, swimming in the pool and playing games."

He was animated when he spoke about the children, and camp. She liked the fact that he was socially conscious.

"And, you?" he asked.

"I run a charity called, 'Like Home.' It's for children and teenagers who have no safe place to go, when leaving dangerous domestic situations, aging out of foster care, those in danger of being trafficked, and those victims of trafficking. I don't want others to struggle, as I struggled. Working with social services, they are placed in home-like situations in groups, and sent to school. It's a cross between an orphanage and foster care. Money isn't involved, and they are safe."

"I heard of it. I didn't know who started it."

"I'm in the background. I haven't spoken in public about my past. Daphne is a mystery, and it's worked well, so far."

"Maybe one day, Daphne will come out to tell her story, as an inspiration to others. Young people need successful role models."

"One day." He made her think. Her career was moving in a different position. Perhaps her life needed to do so, as well.

15

W hen they arrived back at the villa, they parted ways to clean-up and dress for dinner. Daphne showered, put her hair up in a bun, and wrapped a glittery turban on her head. She wasn't in the mood for wigs and heavy makeup. She donned a flowing floral caftan, and glided on to the terrace. Dusk was setting in with the magic hour of an indigo blue sky. The sun was setting on the bay, and the lights of the city below twinkled.

One table was set for two, and River was already seated. He rose upon seeing her, a smile curved on his dimpled face. He looked sexy casual in khaki slacks, a striped shirt, and navy blazer.

"I was told by the wait staff, that it's only us tonight. Everyone else had other plans. The villa is ours for a while," River stated.

"Angie texted me. She and my staff took a limo ride down the coast. Kemsit and Sanjay are dining in town. Paul, Greg, and Riccardo are at their hotels. That leaves us."

"It's a lovely evening and setting. I couldn't think of a better dinner partner. After all, we met at a table for two."

The memory brought a grin to her face, and a tingle down her spine.

River pulled out a chair for her, and she sat. He went back to his seat.

"I want to thank you for inviting me to this delightful place. It's the closest thing I've had to a vacation in years," he said.

"You really are a workaholic?"

"From what I can tell, so are you. Mine is scientific, and yours is creative. At least we love what we do."

"Life is too short to work at something you dislike. We're lucky that we do what we love, and can make a comfortable living at it." She took a deep breath of the sea air. "It feels so good here."

"It's very peaceful."

Leaning into the table, she admitted, "Actually, I'm rather glad that the others aren't here. I don't have to put on my Daphne act. I can enjoy more time as myself."

"I'm glad, too."

A waiter arrived with a bottle of Colli di Salerno. He poured the fizzy red wine into two glasses, and set the bottle on the table before leaving.

"A toast to beauty: Salerno and Meg," River said, meeting her gaze.

She swore that her heart skipped a beat, as she sipped the sweet wine. "Nice."

"Italy knows wine and food." He clinked his glass to hers.

They sipped.

Setting down her glass, she said, "I have to confess that you are the only person I feel comfortable with, and can be myself, instead of some Hollywood actress. With you, I am normal."

"It must be difficult being an actress, and having your life be just another role." He met her gaze, and a tingling warmth filled her body.

"It is. It's exhausting. With you, I don't have to act. Taking that sabbatical in Cairo was good for me. I needed to get back to the real me."

"It's rather funny, isn't it, that by being Daphne or Meg, you are still living a lie."

She tilted her head. "I never really thought of it that way. Daphne is Meg's alter ego, her pseudonym, her other persona. My character." She took a sip of wine. "I am trying to merge them. My next film is the first where I won't be the blonde bombshell. I'm hoping it's the beginning of new, unique roles. I'm tired of being typecast. I'm also getting older. Bombshells have an expiration date."

"Will your fans accept this?"

"It's a chance I have to take, if I want longevity in this business. It's why I formed my own production company. I'm also in talks to do a Broadway play."

"You're in this business for the long run?"

She nodded. "Acting is as necessary as breathing."

He finished off his wine in one gulp, and cleared his throat.

A basket of warm bread, and salads were served.

Daphne wondered what she said that made River go silent. He poured more wine, and his focus moved to the food. When the *pasta e fagioli*, a rich pasta and bean soup, was served, River looked at her, and smiled. The pungent scent of tomatoes and basil wafted in the air.

"The chef is amazing," he said, after taking a spoonful of soup from his bowl.

"He came with the villa. The others don't know what they're missing. The herbs and vegetables come from the gardens."

"*Bellisimo.*"

The main course was clams diablo, with a side of *pasta perciatelli*. Almond limoncello cake was served for dessert.

"How do you stay so thin?" he asked.

"I make two films a year, and once they are released, I celebrate and splurge. Otherwise, it's everything in moderation," she explained, taking a fork full of cake.

"I see."

"After my stint in Cairo, I had to hit my gym, big-time."

"I guess being a Hollywood star is high-maintenance?" he asked.

She tilted her head, wondering what he was driving at. "Not much more than most women, though in Hollywood, image is everything."

He leaned back in his chair, and drew his hand up to his chin, as if sizing her up.

The sound of laughter and voices entered the villa. Kemsit and Sanjay strolled out on the terrace.

"Just in time for dessert?" Kemsit said, flipping her hair over her shoulder.

"Pull up a couple chairs," Daphne invited.

A waiter appeared, and set two chairs at the table, and they sat. He returned with cake and cappuccino.

"This looks incredible," Sanjay commented.

"Did you have fun today?" River asked Sanjay.

"Oh, yes. We strolled down the promenade, but ended up at Fort La Carnale," Sanjay explained. "The castle and museum were quite fascinating."

"The view from the hill was breathtaking," Kemsit added. "We ended up in Old Town, and enjoyed some amazing street food."

"It helped that Kemsit speaks fluent Italian," Sanjay said.

"You do?" Daphne asked.

Kemsit nodded. "A Roman was once part of my life. So very long ago." She gazed out over the terrace, to the sea, seeming to be lost in a memory.

"Gosh, I may be needing you for some interpretation," Daphne said.

"I don't get to speak Italian often." Kemsit sighed.

She had a sip of cappuccino.

"So, what did you do?" Sanjay cocked a bushy eyebrow at River.

"Mmm ... Daphne and I toured the town, incognito. It is a beautiful, historic town."

"It was fun," Daphne added. "All of us are here to have fun."

"Most world premieres are not held in small, foreign towns," Sanjay said.

"We prefer to be different," Daphne said. "The critics, reviewers, and bloggers will still come. The top producer, director, and actress in Hollywood are involved. After all, one of Italy's top actors is my co-star."

"Can't wait to meet Riccardo," Sanjay said. "I loved him in 'Pupone.'"

"I can see you gravitating toward feature films," Daphne commented.

Sanjay chuckled. "Perhaps, one day. For now, it's shorts and documentaries."

After sipping her cappuccino, Daphne had an idea. "I've been considering a documentary on my life, and how my early years relate to my charity. It would be a great way to bring some serious issues to the forefront."

Sanjay leaned forward. "I'm interested."

"Great. Let's brainstorm. Then, we can get together to discuss this project, with my agent, when we get back to the States."

River sighed, and rose. "I want to thank you for a delightful day and evening, Daphne," he said. "You'll have to excuse me. The sea air tires me. I'm going up to my room."

Daphne's smile turned upside down. What a strange ending to such a perfect day. At dinner, he grew quiet, and pensive. Did she say or do something wrong? She thought that they would take an evening stroll. Maybe even a Midnight swim. He was going to bed ... alone?

~

RIVER HAD TO ESCAPE. All of the Hollywood, acting, and schmoozing bullshit was getting on his nerves. That's what he got for getting involved with a famous actress. Yet, he didn't fall in love with a superstar. He fell in love with a decent, fun woman named Meg. Watching her transform from Meg to Daphne, and Daphne to Meg was as exhausting as watching a ping-pong match. How she could handle it was beyond him. It was like dealing with someone who had multiple personality disorder.

He sat out on his suite's balcony, looking out over the illuminated hillside town, and bay beyond. A soft breeze was kicking up, and he drew a deep breath of the cooling night air. What was he doing on the Amalfi Coast in Italy? The scenery was breathtaking, and the town quaint. If not for the invitation, he probably would never have visited. Strolling with Meg brought back old times. Dealing with Daphne and her high-maintenance, jet-setting lifestyle, though, was tense.

All of the decadence overwhelmed him. A private villa with a personal chef? Assistants, stylists, makeup artist, jeweler, agents, publicist? Funny, he was wealthy, and had little staff. At the office, he had employees. At home, he had a housekeeper come in weekly, and a landscape and pool maintenance crew come in weekly to tend to his property. Other than that, he lived a rather simple life. He liked simple. He didn't need a lot of things. He didn't own many things. Earnings were put back in the business, or to his foundation. Helping others meant more than helping himself.

Daphne had a non-profit foundation, but her occupation lent itself to excess. For him, it was over-the-top. For many men, being seen with the world's most famous actress would have been a trophy. He preferred to be with Meg, the waitress who lived above the dress shop, in small town Cairo. He loved the woman with wholesome good looks, and mousy brown hair. Daphne was like an alien. He wasn't looking for a knockout.

He also liked being out of the spotlight. He didn't go into business to become rich and famous. He loved to invent and create. If doing what you loved brought money, so be it. His was a privately-held company. Just like him, private.

He sighed. Tomorrow night, he was Daphne's escort at the movie premiere. In a weak moment, he had agreed to fly to Italy on a whim, to put himself on display. Somehow, he would survive one more night. He would be Daphne's ideal escort, though he wanted Meg. He swallowed hard. He had so much to digest and ponder. On Sunday, he was flying home to the States. He needed to be home.

 s the stretch limousine pulled up to the red carpet, Daphne draw a deep breath, and whispered, "Sparkle, Daphne, sparkle."

"What?" River asked.

She smiled. "It's a ritual when I transition from Meg to Daphne. It's from the book, 'Valley of the Dolls.' Actress Neely says, 'Sparkle,' for confidence. It actually helps."

He laughed. "Sparkle."

"Yes, 'sparkle'. I have to warn you. Be prepared for the deluge. Once we step out, we will be on public display. Everything you say, and do will be fair game for the media."

No matter how many premieres, award shows, and events she attended, Daphne still trembled when exiting the limousine. She felt exposed, naked. She drew another deep breath, in preparation for her greatest acting role, being Daphne.

The door opened, and she slunk out of the limousine. Standing, a barrage of camera flashes and clicks, and a mob of reporters surrounded her. She had selected her gown for this moment. A clinging white confection of crystals and bugle beads, it sparkled like snowflakes. The slit, up- to-there, and plunging neckline, accenting her pale skin, epitomized Daphne. Shimmering on her ears and at her neck were borrowed diamond jewelry. Image was everything. Cheers erupted from the crowd, and her name was called. She winked, flashed her Pepsodent-smile, and waved.

River exited behind her, and came to her side, taking her hand. At that moment, she was comforted. Having someone familiar hold her hand added a degree of warmth. When he squeezed it, her heart rate calmed.

She swiped a stray hair from her platinum wig, away from her flawless face. She side-glanced at River. He was dashing in his black tuxedo. His hair was neatly trimmed, and she realized that, with his classical looks, he could easily be a leading man. He followed her every move with confidence. Having someone who actually cared for her, and whom she cared for, at her side, made the event more tolerable.

They strolled the carpet. In her stiletto sandals, she implemented her famous "wiggle" walk. The snicker on River's face made her smile. He was just learning about Daphne, she thought.

DAPHNE WAS LARGER THAN LIFE, River realized. Hollywood royalty was an understatement. She was worshipped and fawned over like a goddess. He was merely wallpaper at her side, which was fine with him. He didn't know how she could stand all of the groveling. Reporters screamed out questions. Videographers squeezed through crowds for a closer look. Flashes strobed like lightning. The paparazzi annoyed him, but he forced a smile, knowing that he was there to make her look good. He equated the experience with being the queen's date for the senior prom. He was about as necessary. Daphne was the center of the universe, and everything, and everyone revolved around her. She seemed to take it all in stride. He surmised that her familiarity with Red Carpet events made her comfortable. It was just another stage.

She knew when and where to stop, to wink, wave, or blow a kiss. Each action involved a pose, a turn, or a curtsy. She worked the carpet like a politician working a crowd. Cheers erupted. Applause resounded. River followed her lead, following her, as she strutted toward the theater entrance.

Once inside the ornate carved and gilded lobby, with frescoed ceiling, a photography set was against one wall. They were directed to step up on the platform, to pose for formal photographs in front of a *"Mob Boss"* background. Before doing so, Daphne's stylist fluttered by to touch up her hair and makeup, and adjust her gown to make her photo ready. Daphne posed. River was shown where and how to stand. After the photographs were taken, they were escorted to their front row seats.

When the lights went down, and the emcee took the stage, River took a deep breath, and sighed. He was so out of his element. Wearing a tuxedo was uncomfortable, and silly. Being the center of attention was something he loathed. He would have preferred being back at the villa, seated alone, watching the sun set over the bay. Knowing that the evening was just beginning made his head hurt.

The day started out uneventful enough. He went for an early morning solo swim in the villa's pool, that was refreshing. Breakfast was served. He dined alone, as Daphne and her staff were preparing for the big night. She had phone, video, and live interviews with assorted media. After, she was off to a spa for treatments. Upon her return, she had hair and makeup, and gown alterations. He saw her for a fleeting moment. Unlike Meg, Daphne was high maintenance. Being Daphne was a full-time, all-encompassing job.

Where did he fit in, he wondered? Did he fit in?

The film began. He couldn't remember the last time he

actually saw a new theatrical release. Preferring to work on his computer, and in his lab, be found films, concerts, and other entertainment a waste of time. Being a guest, at a movie premiere, he knew he had to pay attention. He was sure that Daphne and others would quiz him on her latest feature. Maybe it would offer some insight into her profession.

He had to admit that the movie was interesting. Daphne did get into character, to play the perfect gangster's moll and hit woman. She was credible, and professional at her craft. Her emotion was riveting. He was sure that it was an award-winning performance. She had found her calling.

AFTER THE MOVIE PREMIERE, a lavish party was set up on a hotel terrace on the beach. Waiters in waistcoats passed out champagne and appetizers, like calamari, cheese, prosciutto, olives, and the like. He nibbled to quell his discomfort. Standing by as Daphne's escort, he had to smile and engage in mindless small talk. She would cast him a glance, and wink. This was her job, not his.

"Would you excuse me?" Daphne asked in her lilting voice. "I need to chat with a producer."

"No problem," he answered, actually glad to be away from the glimmer of her spotlight. He walked across the terrace to a bar.

"Isn't this incredible?" Sanjay asked, stepping beside him. He looked dapper in an ivory tux.

"No," River admitted, with a frown.

"Are you kidding? This is Hollywood royalty."

"It's not my thing." River shrugged. "I feel like the proverbial fish out of water."

"Do you know how many men would love to be in your shoes right now? A movie premiere in Italy, with Daphne?"

"I'm not one of those men. You know me. I'm a geeky loner, who prefers to live a quiet and simple life."

"Surely, I thought that success would bring you out of your shell?" Sanjay ordered a scotch and water.

"Nope. I'm still the same guy." He ordered a glass of white wine.

"Well, you did come this far. That's progress. Thank you for getting me an invitation."

River followed Sanjay away from the bar and the crowd, toward the beach.

"You belong in this crowd, Sanjay. These are your people. You have a future in the business," River explained.

Sanjay nodded. "Thanks to you, Daphne is interested in my producing her documentary."

"Hers is a good cause. The project is worthwhile, and I can see it being very successful. Everything she touches seems to turn to gold."

"Is she turning you into gold, my friend?" Sanjay winked.

River chuckled. "I prefer not to be King Midas."

"She likes you, a lot."

"I like her, a lot, though we live in different worlds. More like different planets. Hey, where's Kemsit?"

"She's making the rounds, observing the event. She finds this entire weekend fascinating. Guests find her fascinating. Hell, I find her fascinating." Sanjay grinned.

"Hmm?"

"Nothing romantic, yet, but we'll keep in touch."

"She's rather mysterious and secretive," River said.

"I like that about her."

"There you are." Daphne appeared, at his side.

River took a sip of his drink.

"I could use one of those." She strode to the bar, and the crowd parted to let her through. A glass of chardonnay was handed to her.

"That's magic," Sanjay whispered to River, before strolling away.

"Dinner is about to be served. We're at the head table with Riccardo, Paul, Greg, and Les. You must meet my agent, Les." She took his arm.

17

Before stepping out of the limousine at the villa, Daphne slipped off her stiletto sandals and let out a sigh.

"Feet hurt?" River asked.

"Too many hours in new shoes," she said, holding the sandals by their thin straps.

The chauffeur opened the door, and she stepped out on the stone walk in her bare feet. The pavement was smooth and warm. She sashayed to the front door, River following. Once inside the foyer, she turned to face him.

"I can't wait to get upstairs and get undressed. This gown is as hot and as tight as being in plastic wrap. Guaranteed, if something is beautiful, its uncomfortable."

"I feel that way about this penguin suit." He reached up to untie the bow tie, and unbutton the two top pearl buttons of his shirt.

She found the way his fingers moved sexy. Biting her lip, she moved toward the stairs. "After we get comfortable, want to meet for a nightcap on the terrace?"

"It's pretty late. I fly out in the morning. I need to back in the office Monday morning," he said.

"It's just a nightcap." She wondered why he was being evasive. All evening he had been rather reserved, going through the motions of being her date. He wasn't the relaxed and fun guy she strolled Salerno with, and shared limoncello.

"I'll meet you on the terrace," he finally agreed.

RIVER WAS SEATED at a bistro table near the balcony, peering out over the illuminated town, with a full moon igniting the bay. His face was silhouetted against the night sky. In jeans and tee shirt, he looked more at ease, and in his element. She approached, glad that she had donned jeans and a tee shirt, as well. Her original idea of wearing just a bath robe seemed presumptuous. As he hadn't been very romantic all evening, she took the hint. Maybe she would find out what was bothering him. Something surely was.

"Lovely evening, isn't it? I'm going to miss the beauty of this place," she said, easing into a chair across from him.

He met her gaze. "I will, too. I have to get back to reality sometime."

"An escape from reality isn't a bad thing."

"Maybe for me, but this is your reality, isn't it?" He scowled.

"I thought that this weekend would be fun for you? Was I wrong?" she asked, concerned.

Sighing, he said, "It's been an interesting experience."

"That's it?" His answer was rather chilly.

"Salerno is beautiful, and I really enjoyed touring the town with you. I could do without all the glitz and glamor, the paparazzi, and the fanfare."

"Movie premieres, galas, and award ceremonies are like that. They are part of my business."

"And your life?"

"Of course, my life."

He looked away, and took a sip of red wine. "Not a part of my life."

She drew a deep breath. That was it. He didn't like the attention and publicity. "I'm sorry. I thought that it would be fun, a change of pace, and a change of scenery."

"I'm not into Hollywood, Daphne. Meg. Whoever you are, tonight."

There was a bite in his voice.

"I'm Meg. With you, I'll always be Meg," she said, raking a hand through her long, mousy brown hair.

He shook his head, taking another sip of wine. After, he took the bottle, poured the red liquid in an empty glass, and handed it to her.

She took the glass. "Thanks. I don't understand."

"Your lifestyle is so erratic. Do you really know who you are? I mean, one moment you're plain and simple Meg. The next, you're some blonde sexpot, Daphne. You have so many projects and deals going on. How do you keep everything straight? Oh, your staff, always at your beck and call. This isn't normal."

"I'm a famous actress. Life isn't normal. It will never be normal."

He took a final slug of his wine, and stood. "I got my answer."

"What are you saying?"

"Tomorrow morning, I am flying back to normal."

"Come on, your life isn't normal, either. You want to live like a tech hermit, yet you are a famous, billionaire businessman. You can't escape who you are, any more than I can escape who I am."

He froze in place, glaring at her.

"We are both the products of our success. My life may be more hectic and public, but neither of us is normal. When we became public figures, that bus left the station," she said.

"At least, I don't have two personas."

She stood to face him. "Don't you? When I met you, you were River, a tow motor operator. Now, you are Rutherford, a tech genius."

"I don't switch back and forth, like Sybil."

"As I had said, Daphne and Meg are merging. No more blonde-bombshell Daphne. Daphne is becoming a more serious actress and movie producer. 'Mata Hari' is just the beginning."

"Gee, another character. How can I keep up?"

"What are you saying?"

"No more characters. Hey, I fell in love with Meg. I don't know this cartoon character, Daphne." He scoffed.

"Cartoon character?" She could feel the color go to her face, as she grew hot in temperature and temperament.

"Jessica Rabbit?" He laughed.

"What?"

"Goodnight, Daphne. Thank you for the entertaining weekend." He turned to leave.

She was trembling. He was brushing her off?

"You're leaving. Just like that?"

He glanced back. "There's nothing left to say."

He disappeared inside. She could hear his footsteps bounding up the marble stairs. Tears swelled in her eyes. He didn't understand. He didn't want to understand. She swallowed the entire glass of wine in one gulp. Maybe, cooler heads would prevail in the morning.

THE NEXT MORNING, Daphne rushed on to the terrace for breakfast. Kemsit was seated, sipping tea. She looked up, and smiled.

"*Buongiorno*," Kemsit greeted.

"Good morning," Daphne answered. "Has River been down yet?"

"River's been gone since dawn. His plane is probably over the Atlantic by now."

"No!" Daphne slunk in a chair.

Kemsit poured her a cup of tea. "Sorry, this isn't stronger, though I'm sure it's five o'clock somewhere."

"I was hoping to catch him before he left. There was so much left unspoken." Daphne sipped the mint tea.

"Lover's quarrel?"

"Lovers? That's a joke," Daphne said. "It's crazy. Most men want to date me because I'm the sexpot, Daphne. River doesn't want to date Daphne, or have anything to do with her."

"He knows that Daphne is just another character?"

"Does he ever? Yet, he can't accept it."

"Maybe, some time away will give him time to think?"

"Kemsit, I can only hope."

"I always say, that if it is meant to be, love will find a way. Better not to dwell on it, and just live."

Daphne drew a deep breath of the fresh sea air.

"I hope that you had a fun weekend?" Daphne asked, meeting her friend's gaze.

"Very much. I haven't been to Italy in years. It brings back many memories, and has created new ones."

"Like Sanjay?"

Kemsit tossed back her head of wavy black hair. "He's a good man, but I'm not looking for a relationship. We left as friends. Sometimes, it is much better that way."

"I see your point"

"He and River left for the airport together."

Daphne swallowed hard. "Well, when we get back to L.A., we begin filming the dance scenes. I know that you need to get back to Cairo. Thankfully, movies aren't made in sequence."

"I'm looking forward to seeing you transform into Mata Hari."

Another character, Meg thought.

18

When River arrived home, he was greeted with a repeat of the frenzy that had erupted when Meg's identity as Daphne ,was first revealed in Cairo. This time, the media projected photographs of he and Daphne at the *"Mob Boss"* premiere. From the local *Cairo News,* national broadcasts and press, to the entertainment channels, he had Daphne were an item. He should have been prepared. All of the press and paparazzi snapped enough photographs at the premiere. So much for wanting to return to normal, as a hermit loner. As long as he was with Daphne, his life would be in the public eye. There was no escaping her larger-than-life persona. He realized that her disguise as Meg was short-lived, and that the press would now recognize him. Together, they would be on display.

His heart hurt. For the first time in his life, a woman had touched his heart, and penetrated his soul. Time spent with Meg was never enough. Yet, Meg was Daphne. Daphne was a caricature. He had fallen in love with demure Meg, not bombshell Daphne. The two were intertwined.

He leaned back in his office chair, staring blankly at his

computer screen. An image of he and Daphne on the Red Carpet peered back. Rubbing the bridge of his nose, he closed his eyes. Whatever possessed him to rush off to Italy? He wasn't a compulsive person. Didn't he know that attending a movie premiere, as the escort to the world's most famous actress, would bring unwanted publicity? Was one lovely afternoon, strolling through Salerno with Meg, worth it? Swallowing hard, he opened his eyes to the difficult truth. No.

His smartphone rang. Luke.

"Hello," he greeted.

"Hey, Buddy, keeping secrets? Running off to Italy without telling anyone," Luke said, and chuckled.

"It was spare-of-the-moment."

"That's so not like you. How was it?"

"Exhausting. I also learned that I'm not into the Hollywood lifestyle."

"You sure looked the part."

"Actually, it was like a part, an acting role." He pondered. Yes, an acting role, like Daphne's.

"You're the envy of every man in town. Well, except me. I have Sara. Being in Italy for the weekend, with the famous Daphne is like a male fantasy come true."

"It wasn't what you think. It was all business, her acting business, and no romance."

"Really?"

"Fact. Going was a mistake. Now, I have to pay the price, with all of this unwanted publicity."

"Hey, you're now a role model for all the reclusive nerds out there. There's hope that they can land a famous and beautiful woman."

"I never wanted to 'land' a famous woman. I fell for Meg, not Daphne."

"That is a problem."

"Big problem. I just want this publicity to die down, so I can go back to my boring normal life. No more movie stars or Hollywood."

"Never say never."

"Never."

THE SOUNDSTAGE WAS SET to resemble a Parisian theater, with gilded pillars, ornate frescoes and crystal chandeliers. The red velvet seats were filled with extras, in their 1900's tuxedos, evening gowns, and feather coifs. The raised stage was framed by red velvet curtains. A Javanese percussion musical ensemble, a *Gamalon*, was set up, practicing their hypnotic tinkling music and chants. Bronze gongs, zither, flute, drums, and metallophones, were hammered, while hands slapped percussion.

Daphne stood in the wings with Kemsit. Her sheer, nude body stocking, flecked with rhinestones, was covered with a flowing emerald slit silk skirt, with a clear and emerald rhinestone, fringed hip belt. Her bra was matching sparkling rhinestones with fringe. An ornate necklace, drop earrings, and armbands added interest. A draped rhinestone headpiece covered her upswept, newly-dyed black hair. Dramatic makeup lined her eyes, her lips a deep red. She was wrapped in a filmy golden veil.

"Why am I nervous?" Daphne asked Kemsit. A shiver crawled up her spine.

"Because every great performer gets the jitters before a show. You are well-rehearsed."

She drew a deep breath. "And, I know that there can, and will be retakes. I think it's because this is more than dancing. Mata Hari leaned toward burlesque. Stripping off everything is a bit intimidating. I have never appeared nude in a film."

"You have a body stocking, and Mata Hari only revealed her nudity for a moment."

"I know."

"We rehearsed this. Let your heart take over. Dance from the heart, not the brain."

"From the heart and the soul," Daphne repeated.

"Now, take a few deep breaths. Listen to the music. You *are* Mata Hari, the most sensual dancer on the planet. Feel the music. Dance with your soul. Her soul."

Daphne closed her eyes, and took a few breaths.

I am Mata Hari.

On cue, she pranced on to the stage like a Javanese princess, in her bare feet, the veil covering her face and her flowing costume. She spun around several times. On the final spin, she draped the veil behind her, revealing her ornate costume. Playing with the veil, she performed butterflies and whirlpools. Tossing the veil forward, she caught it on her neck. Using her hands, she lifted the knotted veil above her head, in a bondage move, while dancing figure eights. Removing the veil, she spun it on the floor, like a cobra ready to strike. The audience ooh'ed and ahh'ed.

Tossing the veil aside, she continued to dance levels of figure eights with her hips, rib cage, head, and arms. Moving on to outward eights, alternating her hips and rib-cage, she traversed the stage. Snake arms. Head glides. Javanese finger ripples and waves. Slow and sensuous, like the music.

While turning, she released her skirt. Waving it around like a matador's cape, she tossed it to the side. The hip belt remained, fringe swirling as she shimmied her hips and chest. She spun around, tossing her hair, until it was released to her shoulders, the headpiece in place, like a crown.

The music slowed even more. Camel walk undulations and body waves, adding belly rolls to the mix. She slid her hands up her legs, outlining her body, to her chest. With a back bend, she descended to the floor. Undulating like a quivering serpent, her head kissed the floor, and reached forward. Up and down. Pulling in her legs, she tossed her hair to and fro.

Rising, her back to the audience, the removed the hip belt, and flung it toward the wings. The outline of her derriere, encased in rhinestones, was revealed. She flung off the bra to gasps from the audience. She spun around, facing front for a brief moment, and danced off the stage.

Thunderous applause erupted, with shouts and whistles. Even after the director called, "Cut," the theater shook with the sound.

Kemsit helped her into an *abaya*, a robe, and she stepped on to the stage. More applause.

"Well?" she called out.

The director approached the stage. "Just wow! In one take. I can't imagine that being repeated. It was truly an out-of-body experience. If Mata Hari were that amazing, I can see why she climbed to fame and fortune."

Daphne curtsied, and smiled. "Thank you."

The audience stood in an ovation.

She curtsied again.

The director shook his head, and swiped at his brow. "Truly remarkable."

"Did the cameras get steamed up?" Daphne asked, with a giggle.

"I think the crew got hot and bothered," Kemsit whispered to Daphne.

"Ladies, you rock. Take a break. We can do the next dance scene this evening," the director said, with a broad smile.

Daphne swept off the stage with Kemsit.

"I really was possessed when I danced. I don't remember much," Daphne admitted.

"You were in 'the zone,' and that's great. You danced from your soul."

"I did. Thank you for choreographing, and setting the mood. The musicians were amazing."

"Shall we practice tonight's duet?" Kemsit asked.

"Good idea. I'll change out of this costume, or what there is left of it." She walked toward her dressing room, Kemsit following.

Daphne was excited to not only have Kemsit choreograph and orchestrate her dances, but to have her perform a duet in the film. She wanted to do something special for her. Kemsit resisted at first, but the director loved the idea, and convinced her. Theirs would be the first dance scene in the finished movie. Kemsit created a Javanese inspired temple dance, complete with ankle bells.

The other dance sequences were snippets of dance vignettes in different costumes and settings for inclusion later in the film. Those sequences had been filmed the previous day. Her just-performed solo was the major dance performance of the film.

"Well, this is my last part in this movie," Kemsit said. "After this duet, I can go home."

"I'm going to miss you. You have no idea how you made this movie possible."

"I just helped. You have channeled the essence of Mata Hari. I can't wait to view the final product."

"Another movie premiere." Daphne put a finger to her lips. "Perhaps, in Paris?"

"You tempt me. I love Paris."

19

"Paris? What the hell?" River asked aloud, grasping an embossed invitation in his hand.

He shook his head. Couldn't Daphne take a hint? He was not interested in participating in anything that had to deal with Hollywood and the film industry. Yes, it was the first film produced by her production company. It was her debut as a character, other than a blonde sexpot. She was the mysterious and dark-haired dancer and spy, Mata Hari. This project and role were important to her.

After Italy, he did finally agree to talk to her. He expressed his interest in Meg, but not Daphne. She listened, but he knew that she didn't understand. He explained his disdain for being in the limelight, and in the tabloids. The Hollywood carousel was her world, but not his. He was content to create and invent, in anonymity. Though disappointed, she still maintained a friendship for over six months. Her Mata Hari film project took her around the world, from the Netherlands to France. Meanwhile, he worked on new drone technology, and autonomous aviation. Though they were entrenched in their separate worlds, she still sent an invitation.

Sanjay called. "Hey, River, *Bonjour*."

"No. Just, no."

"What are you saying? You did get invited to the Paris premiere of '*Mata Hari*?'"

"Yes, but I'm not going."

"You're turning down Daphne? This is her role of a lifetime."

"Her role, not mine. Let her shine in the spotlight, alone."

"River, it's only for a weekend. You seemed to enjoy Italy."

"Salerno. Not the Hollywood schmoozing. Not the paparazzi. I won't be featured in every newspaper and magazine around the world. The publicity has finally dwindled, after Italy. I like my peace and quiet."

"You are crazy. How many men would turn down Daphne?"

"One. Me."

"River?"

"Have a great time. Kemsit's going."

"I know. She landed a part in the movie. Oh, and I've begun working with Daphne on her documentary about her life, and 'Like Home' foundation. She's incredible."

"I'm glad that Hollywood is working out for you. It's just not my thing. Wish Daphne much success."

After he hung up, River poured himself a stiff drink. Life was simpler before he met Meg.

RIVER READ about the premiere in the papers, and saw it in the media. Instead of his face flashed all over the place, Daphne and Kemsit graced the pages and screens. They walked the Red Carpet together in glamorous Middle Eastern *baladi* dresses. Strategic cutouts, bugle beads, crystals and fringe accented every curve and movement. Their long, dark hair shimmered, ornate headdresses adding accent. The intricate eye makeup, and red lips accented their features. He knew that they outdid the infamous Mata Hari.

"A heck of a lot better than being with me," he muttered. "Smart film promotion."

He sat back to read reviews of the film.

"Seductive. Sensual. Mata Hari comes to life in vivid detail. Incredible dance," reviews read.

"Daphne has raised the bar. Her transformation from blonde bombshell to dark-haired seductress is nothing less than incredible," another reviewer wrote.

"Golden Globe and Oscar material," yet another stated.

River sat back. Sounded like her new endeavor was a smash hit. He was happy for her. Her dreams were coming true. The career she had worked so hard to attain was paying off. Her career was her life. He hoped that she was happy.

DAPHNE WAS EXHAUSTED, after the whirlwind weekend in Paris for the *"Mata Hari"* premier. After arriving home on Tuesday morning, she remained in her nightgown and robe all day. Refusing all telephone calls and communication, she plopped on her living room sofa to drink tea, and pore over movie reviews. The reviews were positive. Actually, they were the best she had ever received for any of her films. Her transition from blonde sex kitten to serious actress seemed to be a success. The foray into producing also proved to be a hit. There were also many comments about her seductive dancing.

"I took a chance, and danced," she said, and laughed, borrowing from Kemsit's dance quote.

If not for visiting Cairo, and studying with Kemsit, the project wouldn't have happened. The rash decision to take a sabbatical from her career, changed her life. Kemsit was instrumental in the movie being a success. Her choreography and costuming help were invaluable. Walking the Red Carpet together was genius. It set the tone for the film. The publicity was beyond expectations. She also made a very good friend. On Sunday, she and Kemsit toured Paris, enjoyed tea at the Ritz, and shopped the Place de Vendome. That evening, Kemsit caught connecting flights home. Daphne flew out on Monday.

The weekend was a swirl of activity, but something was missing. Rather, someone. On Saturday, after lunch with her guests, she would have preferred to have walked the cobbled streets of Monmarte, and climb the stairs of the Tour Eiffel with River. Instead, incognito, she explored by herself. She realized that through most of her life, she was alone. Yes, she was occupied with staff, the accoutrements of the film business, and the press, but during time off, she was alone. Everyone seemed to pair off, except her. Even Kemsit had Sanjay. She sighed.

The world's most famous actress didn't have a date, or a significant other. She never met the right person. Men pursued Daphne, the kittenish, sexy actress. They didn't want to hold intelligent conversations, or explore her soul. Men just wanted arm candy. Dating her was a trophy. Their motives were purely sexual. Contrary to what her image projected, she was not promiscuous, far from it. She spent her weekends, and her nights, alone. Immersing herself in her career became the focus of her life.

Meeting River changed things. Meeting someone she thought was an ordinary man, who didn't know who she was, had been refreshing. There were no motives or expectations. He didn't care if she were a waitress. He enjoyed her company for who she was, not what she was. Even after revealing their secrets, he viewed her as an equal. More than that, he wasn't impressed by her fame, and certainly not her fortune.

Other famous actresses dated, and even married men outside of the film business, with success. Meryl Streep was married to a sculptor for over forty years. He attended her Red

Carpet events, without objection. Yet, River abhorred Hollywood, the film business, and related obligations. How could she be with someone so unsupportive? *"Mata Hari"* was her most important project, to date. Yet, he wouldn't attend the premiere.

She wondered if he would attend the United States' premiere, if it were in his backyard. She did something completely unorthodox. Her production staff was in Cairo, working out the logistics for the event to be held in the small town. She convinced her public relations staff, that a town named Cairo, was a perfect setting. Les, her manager, agreed. Kemsit, the film's choreographer, and dancer had a studio there. The town was also the location of Daphne's infamous escape from the limelight. There were so many story angles.

LUKE WAS the first person to share the news. River was not happy.

"What are you saying? Hollywood scouts are in town planning for the United States premiere of 'Mata Hari,' here? Why in Cairo?" River asked, seated at the lunch counter of the Belle Diner with Luke.

"Daphne. It's her production, and production company," Luke replied, taking a bite of his club sandwich.

"Why, here?"

Luke shrugged. "Why not here. The town has an exotic name, Cairo. Daphne put it on the map, when she escaped here as Meg. Plus, Kemsit's studio is here. There's a lot of publicity to be had."

"When I learn the date, I'm flying out of here. Let Daphne have her fun." He sipped his strawberry milkshake, suddenly wishing it were something stronger.

"Come on, River. Why escape? I'm sure she wants you here."

"Precisely."

"You know, You're crazy." Luke stared at him.

"What?"

"You will never have a normal relationship, you do know that?"

"What are you saying?"

"You live like a hermit, and are married to your job. That would drive most women nuts. Daphne, on the other hand, isn't normal, either. She's married to her career. Neither of you have expectations, and are not needy. It would be the perfect arrangement. You could have your careers, yet find time to be together. Quality time. So, you go to some of her events, and she attends yours. Big deal. Relationships are all give and take."

River shook his head. Was Luke kidding?

"You know that I practically live at the shop all week. Sara teaches, and has Rick. We spend weekends together as a family. We have careers, and a life. It works."

"Sara's not the world's most famous actress."

"I'm not one of the world's tech geniuses. You complement each other. It could work."

River's head was spinning. Why was Luke making sense?

"Why don't you try to make it work? A long-distance romance could be successful. Heck, both of you have private planes at your disposal."

"You're saying that I should attend the Cairo premiere with Daphne?"

"At least talk to her. You know, love is not easy to find, especially for you. Why throw it away?"

River sighed. "Daphne isn't Meg."

"Yes, she is. Actually, she's better than Meg. A waitress would end up bored to death with you."

"Thanks a lot."

Luke winked. "I know you."

"Better than I know myself," River muttered.

RIVER DECIDED to take Luke's advice, some of it. He agreed to attend the United States' premier of *'Mata Hari,'* in Cairo. However, he declined her invitation to be Daphne's escort on the Red Carpet. As at the European premiere, Kemsit would join her, and the public relations would be priceless. She could be the star, while he faded into the crowd.

The King Tut was selected to host the film premiere, and after-party. The venue was as exotic and ostentatious as the film. After the film's showing, Kemsit, her dance companies, and Middle Eastern band would provide the party's entertainment. Stage performances, dance lessons, and a dance party, *hafla*, would keep with the film's dance theme.

In discussing the event, Daphne shared a plan. At first, River thought it was preposterous. The more she explained, the more it made sense.

"I'm tired of parties, small talk, and having to 'sparkle,'" Daphne explained.

"Interesting. I thought you thrived on it," he said.

"It's business, not a personal choice. In Cairo, everyone will be preoccupied with the entertainment and activities. I'm sure that I can slip away, unnoticed. Guests will think that I'm backstage with the dancers."

"Slip away?" He was intrigued.

"With you."

He swallowed hard.

"Me?"

"I can tell my table mates that I'm going backstage to see my old friends. Once there, I can change into 'Meg clothes.' Kemsit and her ladies will keep my secret. After, I will sneak into the kitchen, and out the back, kitchen door. No paparazzi will be there, I'm sure. If they were, they'd think I was just the hired help."

"And?"

"You will be waiting in your beater car. No one will recognize us. We can park behind the Classy Chassis. Estelle will keep my secret. I still have a key to the apartment."

"And?"

"We can finally be alone ... to chat."

"You make it sound so simple. What makes you think that all of these women will keep your secret? No one will notice us?"

"Kemsit and her dancers have a bond. It's a sisterhood built on trust."

"Interesting." He still had his doubts.

"Won't they miss you at the party?"

"Kemsit can give my regrets, and tell people that I wasn't feeling well, and went back to my hotel room."

River pondered her idea. What did he have to lose? Maybe, Luke was right. He needed to discuss the viability of a long-distance relationship. This could be the opportunity he needed.

DAPHNE THOUGHT that she was out of her mind, actually thinking that she could pull off this stunt. So far, everything had gone without a hitch. Before the film was shown, she stood in the spotlight, providing an introduction to the documentary. In her sapphire, bugle bead and crystal *baladi* gown, she glimmered under the spotlight. After her presentation, applause resounded, and she sashayed off stage.

She sat in the front row with her co-stars and crew, to view the film. Watching herself on the screen always made her squirm. She always found something to criticize, little things that no one else seemed to notice. After premieres, she never revisited a film, or performance. Instead, she focused on the next project.

When the film ended, she took her bow, and regaled in the spotlight and applause. As the band began to play, everyone's focus turned to the tantalizing appetizers, served by the King Tut's robed wait staff, and the Arabic band playing on the stage. She excused herself, without any objection. Sanjay, who was in on the plan, was seated at the main table, to provide any cover.

Daphne winded her way to the backstage dressing room. Kemsit and her dancers were doing last-minute primping for their performances. After removing her cosmetics, Daphne had a dancer arrange a *hijab*, headscarf on her head. Without make-up, and hiding her hair, she looked like any ordinary Muslim woman. The long-sleeved tunic, slacks, and sandals added to the disguise. Kemsit assured her that no one would recognize her. The other dancers agreed.

When she exited the kitchen door, she approached River's old car. He smirked, rolling down the window.

"Can I help you?" he asked, visibly annoyed.

"It's me, Daphne. Meg."

His eyes grew wide, and he chuckled. "You had me fooled. Get in."

She slipped into the car. Drawing a deep breath, she sighed.

"How'd it go?" he asked, pulling out of the parking lot.

"Went off without a hitch. No one recognized me."

As they drove on to the main street, they passed a swarm of paparazzi and fans at the entrance of the King Tut. No one so much as glanced at them. Entering the city limits of downtown Cairo, the streets were quiet. The globed street lamps beamed down on empty sidewalks. The businesses were closed, as the focus was on the King Tut, not on the town.

After parking behind The Classy Chassis, they strolled to the door leading up to the upstairs' apartment. Estelle had left the brass lamp on in the bay window. Daphne smiled. She was, in a way, coming home. Unlocking the glass door, and climbing the narrow stairs, reminded her of her sabbatical. That little apartment had been a special place. She knew that if she ever returned to Cairo, she had to revisit. She continued to pay the rent, for that reason. Returning with River made her feel like she was just plain Meg.

"Brings back memories, huh?" River asked, as they reached the upstairs landing.

She beamed. "Fond memories."

Unlocking the door, and stepping on to the parquet, she glanced about the small space, as if entering a time capsule. The chairs, and table with the brass lamp, the coffee table, green sofa, where she slept, and tan carpet were the same. River followed her inside.

"Some things stay the same," he said. "I can't believe that you kept it."

"This is my little piece of Heaven. I just wanted to hold on to it for a bit."

She laughed, walking through the living room and down the narrow hall. He trailed behind.

"I did leave in a bit of a hurry." Her suitcases and clothes were strewn on the bedroom floor where she had left them. Even her toothbrush and cosmetics remained on the bathroom counter. The scent of her floral perfume still hung in the air. The extra room still had the quaint African animals on the walls.

In the kitchen, she opened the refrigerator.

"Thank goodness Estelle cleaned out the food. She did leave bottled water, and added this." She removed a bottle of champagne.

"And, these." River pointed to two champagne flutes set on the counter.

"She did think of everything."

"Give me that," he said.

She handed him the bottle of champagne. He unwrapped the foil and wire cage. Taking a nearby towel, he popped open the cork, and promptly poured the frothing liquid into the flutes.

"To a delightful reunion," he said, handing her a glass.

She took it, frothy foam drizzling down her fingers. They clinked glasses, and sipped.

"It's so calm, and peaceful here. No staff. No itineraries. Small and intimate. Personal." She sighed, the memories of her brief sabbatical, a collage flashing through her mind.

"When you were Meg."

She turned her head to meet his gaze. "I'm still Meg. For you, I'll always be Meg."

"I'm trying hard to accept that. I really am trying." He took another sip of champagne.

Meg pointed to the living room, where River followed, and joined her on the sofa.

"I know that you dislike the Hollywood scene. Heck, I know little about technology. We're even. So what? Other actresses have private lives, as do techies. A career doesn't define a person."

"I've been telling myself that. Our worlds are different, yet, I suppose, anything is possible with effort."

She heard him sigh. He set his flute on the coffee table.

"Are you finally understanding how to differentiate our business, from our personal lives? I know that mine seem to be intertwined, but they really aren't. I can adjust to make things work for us." There, she said it. "Relationships are give and take, and I have to learn how to give.

"I have to admit that I've been a bit of a hypocrite, chastising you for your dedication to your career, while I have been as addicted to mine. I can adjust, as well."

Meg set her glass on the coffee table. Meeting his emerald gaze, she said, "I love you, River, and I want this to work."

He looped his arm around her shoulders, making her tingle with warmth. "We can make this work. It may take setting up boundaries, making some sacrifices, and logging in some serious flight time."

"This is all new for me," she admitted. "I haven't been in a relationship for years."

"Years? You?" He raised an eyebrow.

"Daphne is a fantasy. Meg is not as desirable." She shrugged.

"I find Meg irresistible." He squeezed her shoulders.

Tears formed in her eyes. The last time she fell in love, it was with a co-star in an early film. She mistook sexual chemistry for love, and had her heart broken. This was more than chemistry. River was a fascinating person; intelligent, motivated, fun, and sexy without trying.

"I love you," he said is a whisper. "Both of you."

He made her smile.

Drawing her in to his arms, he held her close, and snug. He lowered his head and his lips met hers in a gentle kiss, the touch of his lips, sending shockwaves down her spine. She kissed him back, and the intensity of his kisses increased. Parting her lips, she welcomed his tongue to mingle with hers. The warm, salty dance made her head spin. She was falling into him, and under his spell.

He drew away. "I want you. If you had a bed, I'd carry you off to it."

"You are in my bed, already."

"Huh?"

"I slept on this sofa."

He chuckled.

"Yes, really."

"Hmm." He tilted his head, as if sizing up the sofa.

She leaned back into a pillow set against the arm rest, and lifted her legs up, on to the cushions. "There."

Taking the cue, he moved up and over her, his arms cradling her. Heat enveloped her, as his body heat contacted hers. His spicy scent and rising passion were intoxicating. She wrapped her legs around him, drawing him closer.

"This would be a lot more fun if our clothes weren't in the way," he said, in a breathy whisper.

"I'm sure we can make that happen."

THE NEXT MORNING, Meg awakened, curled up in River's arms on the green sofa. He was sound asleep, exhaling puffs of breath. She squeezed out of his arms, and the tight space without disturbing him. Her gaze lingered over his naked form, curled sideways against the back of the sofa. He was impressive, even without clothing, sinewy muscle and definition. Rubbing her eyes, she giggled at memories of the night before. Who needed a bed?

She padded to the bathroom. A shower was in order. As the warm water pelted her face, she thought about the past. After Alejandro, she wondered if she could ever trust another man with her body, and her heart. She learned how to draw the line between making films, and real life. Acting was merely a business. No more emotional attachment with co-stars. For a scene, she could turn passion on and off, just as she could, tears. Fellow actors found it baffling how she could ignite the screen, and turn off the switch when the scene was over. She was proud of her skill.

She feared that it would affect her personal life. With River, it was different. Everything she felt, and did, was real. Everything came from the heart, and the depths of her soul. Her fear of being unable to relate to the opposite sex in a natural way, was unfounded. She wasn't acting. The progression from friends to lovers was organic. Love was supposed to be like this, wasn't it?

After, she dressed in clothes from a suitcase; leggings, a

flowing tunic and headscarf. She packed her two suitcases, and carried them to the front door, setting them down.

"Where are you going?" River's voice called.

She glanced back, to meet his gaze, as he peered over the back of the sofa.

"Nowhere, yet. Just putting my suitcases by the door," she answered.

"You're not coming back?"

"To this apartment, no. Someone else needs to make memories here. It shouldn't be unoccupied."

"I see." His voice was low.

"I'm not leaving you. I'll be coming back to see you." She walked toward the sofa. Bending down she wrapped her arms around him, and kissed him squarely on the lips.

"That's good to know."

"I'm not leaving you," she assured. She swore to herself that she never would.

"I better get showered and dressed. We have a fun day ahead."

"We do?"

He nodded, with a wide grin. "I'm taking you to 'The Farm,' where I work and play."

CALLING THE SPRAWLING ACREAGE A FARM, was an understatement. There were the stereotypical white clapboard home with black shutters and wraparound front porch, and a large red wood barn and outbuildings. However, there were no animals or crops.

Entering the front door of the farmhouse, she expected to see antiques and calico. Instead, the interior had been opened up, and reconfigured into a contemporary showcase. Modular furniture, in hues of white, tan, and navy blue filled the space. Accent rugs in colorful diagonal designs covered the original wide plank floors. Glass tables had stone pedestals. Figurative sculpture and abstract wall art added interest.

"Welcome to my home," River waved his arms.

"It's interesting ... like you."

She scanned the space as she walked around. Perusing the kitchen, she noted how pristine it was. The stainless-steel appliances, even the massive range hood, appeared shimmering new. The black granite countertops were devoid of accessories, save for a coffee maker.

"As you can tell, I don't cook," he said.

"I can tell."

"I had the house gutted, and redesigned it myself. It's a 'smart home,' with the latest technology. Everything is automated, and can be controlled from my watch, phone, pad, or computer. Instead of window coverings, layers of glass contain filaments, that make them go opaque at the touch of a button. That wall across from us may appear to be flat white. However, with the touch of a button, it becomes a monitor for movies, television, or computer."

He demonstrated the wall and windows with his phone. Daphne was mesmerized.

"My home is part of my working lab."

"Interesting."

"Let me show you around."

He led her on a tour of his unique home. Every aspect had a technology aspect. From the temperature-controlled bath and shower, beds with mattresses that could adjust firmness, warmth, angle, and vibration, everything was computer-controlled. Daphne found is fascinating, but intimidating.

"I don't know if I want my house to be smarter than me," she said.

He chuckled.

.   .   .

THE BIG RED barn was his "think tank" and laboratory. The barn had been converted into offices, classrooms, a kitchen, and upstairs bunk and bathroom facilities. What was once a riding arena, was now a "clean room" computer automation laboratory.

"This is where we create robotics and other artificial intelligence."

"You enjoy making humans obsolete?"

"Making lives easier for humans, so they don't have to work so hard, so they can have more time for play." He winked.

He demonstrated human-like robots programmed to clean floors, dust, wash windows, and pick up objects.

"Robots can do everything that a human can," he said.

"Everything?"

"Yes. There are some amazing lifelike sex robots, that can do everything." He winked.

"Now, that's creepy."

"Not really."

She stared at him.

"Having a sex robot is far safer than a hooker, or a one-night stand."

He said it with a straight face, that made her flinch.

Putting his arm around her shoulders, he whispered, "No, I'm not into it. A robot couldn't take the place of you. Don't worry."

"That's good to know."

"There's a market for everything."

SPENDING the morning and early afternoon with River was educational. Learning about his business made her realize how intelligent he really was. He was a tech genius. Their animated conversation continued on the ride to her hotel. He parked the beater in the lot, retrieved her suitcases from the trunk, and they walked together in the lobby. Paparazzi and media were lingering in the lobby, and at the hotel bar. None noticed them. The baggy clothes and *hijab* provided a perfect disguise. River's beard growth, jeans and faded flannel shirt made him appear unkept, and unimportant.

"May I help you?" a hotel employee asked, with raised brows.

"We have a room here," Daphne said, waving her key card, and putting it back in her pocket.

"Okay. Enjoy your stay," the man said, and walked away.

River took her hand, and they walked to a bank of elevators, and entered one, alone. Daphne slid her key card in a special slot that allowed access to the penthouse floor. Exiting the elevator, they were met by security.

"Stop. This is a private floor," the burly uniformed guard bellowed.

Daphne smiled, pulled off her head scarf, shook her hair, and faced him.

He squinted. "Miss Daphne?"

She answered in her kittenish voice, and sashayed down the hall, to her suite. Once inside, she sighed.

"Good job," River said, setting down her bags.

"Trust me, it gets old."

He glanced about her suite, and shrugged. "Typical presidential suite."

The seating area with fireplace, baby grand piano, stocked bar, dining room, conference table, and wall monitor were found in most luxury suites. An open door revealed a bedroom beyond.

She nodded. "Hotel suites do look the same. Sometimes, I forget what city or town I'm in."

"It's why I prefer to stay home, and sleep in my own bed."

"I wish I had that luxury." Her job demanded travel for work and promotional purposes.

"So, tonight, you're speaking, and taking questions at a Town Hall meet and greet, in the high school auditorium?" he asked.

"I promised the mayor that I'd do something to mingle with the citizens of Cairo. I'm actually looking forward to it. Better yet, after, Kemsit is hosting a party at her studio for her dancers and dance companies. I can't wait to see everyone again, and dance."

"You leave for L.A. in the morning?"

"Yes, back to reality."

The reality was that she would be leaving him, and returning to her whirlwind Hollywood life.

"It's your turn to come out and visit me. You haven't seen my house, yet."

20

A t lunch hour, as he bit into a Rueben sandwich, while seated at his desk, River clocked on the news on his monitor. He had such a hectic morning, that he ordered in, and planned on working while eating. On a whim, he thought that he'd catch up on current events.

The photograph of Daphne flashed on the screen, as the anchorwoman began to speak. Curious, he turned up the volume.

"Daphne, the most famous face in the world, has been called out as a fraud. A homeless woman, claiming to be her estranged mother, has come forward with allegations of abuse and abandonment, by her famous daughter."

A film clip of a woman in tattered clothing, with unkept hair, and smudges of dirt on her ruddy face, appeared. She was being quizzed by reporters.

"I thought it was about time the world learned the truth about my daughter. She never talks about her past, for a reason. I ain't got much, but whatever I had, I spent on her. I waitressed and cleaned toilets to pay for her acting lessons. I lived in the projects, but I gave her a home, and food on the table. I have nothing to show for it. When she became rich and famous, what did she do? She disowned me. She pretended not to know me. Didn't give me a dime. I got sick, and she never returned my calls for help. I ended up on the streets. She don't care. She don't care about nobody but herself," the woman explained, with tears glossing over her hollow eyes.

"Why did you just decide to come forward, now?" the reporter asked.

The woman cleared her throat, and rubbed her nose in her sleeve. "Someone came snooping around, something about filming a documentary on her life. Never asked me nothing. Well, someone had to tell the truth. I'm her mamma."

The clip ended, and the news anchor continued, "Daphne's office was contacted, and has no comment at this time. The mystery of Daphne's past may be solved, shedding light on her character, or lack of. This story is not going away any time soon."

River leaned forward, glaring at the screen. What the hell? This was not the story Daphne told him. She said that she ran away from a neglectful and abusive situation, worked to send herself to acting classes, and struggled on her own, since her teens. She had lost contact with her mother, a supposed drug addict, years before.

He drew a deep breath, and dialed her private cell phone number.

Daphne answered, breathless. "Hello."

"It's River. What's going on?"

She cleared her throat, sounding like she had been crying. "I'd like to know. That woman is not my mother. She's a fraud. My mother never spent a dime on me. She treated me as if I never existed. When I left, she never looked for me. I never heard from her."

"Are you sure?"

"Of course, I'm sure. Why won't anyone believe me?" She

sniffled. "Sanjay found her grave, while conducting research for my documentary."

"Your real mother is dead? You can discredit this imposter?" he asked, a strange sense of relief washing over him.

"I plan on it. It's just that she's ruining my reputation, in the meantime. She's making me out to be some evil daughter."

"Are you being helped?"

"Les, Angie, and my publicist are on it. Can you believe that she has an attorney representing her? She wants to sue me for negligence, and elder abuse?"

"That's absurd. Sounds like she smells money."

"I have money, but my reputation is at stake. If the public doubts me, and turns against me, I'm ruined." Her voice was trembling.

"The faster she's discredited, the better."

"I know. Her attorney is trying to drag this out, and milk it for all it's worth. Already, the papers are equating me with Mata Hari, a cold and ruthless opportunist. It's awful."

"Sanjay's documentary will set things straight."

"It's nowhere ready for release. It's what caused this woman to come out of the woodwork. She heard about it, and decided to jump on the bandwagon for personal gain."

"What can I do? I can fly out tonight." He wanted to do something.

"There's nothing you can do."

"I'm flying out, anyway. I won't have you facing this alone," he insisted.

DAPHNE HID behind the walls of her compound, pacing the rooms in her mansion. Up until this point, her ten years of success were devoid of scandal. How dare a woman claiming to be her mother come forward to ruin her life? Instead of contacting her personally, this imposter created a media spectacle.

When she left the projects, Meg never returned, or looked back. She had an absentee mother, and strung-out siblings. She grew up like a weed, on her own. No one was concerned about where she went, or what she did. Her mother and sisters only worried about their next hit of drugs and sexual encounter. Her mother liked the extra money from the check she received every month from the government, as each child and grandchild increased the payout. She never spent a dime on Margaret, yet alone paid for acting lessons. Through the years, no one ever contacted her. She was certain that they had no idea that Daphne was the Margaret. Her life was so far-removed from theirs.

Sanjay researched her past, to add a personal angle to the documentary on her charity. Throughout his investigation, he never encountered anyone claiming to be a member of her family. He did visit a pauper's cemetery, where he visited and photographed a grave that appeared to be her mother's. Buried in the plot was Marion Lynn Miller, with a description, and birthdates that matched Daphne's recollection. She died of a heroin overdose. The discovery offered closure. As for her sisters, Sanjay found nothing. Daphne assumed that they met, or would meet the same fate. They were much older than she, and she never interacted with them while growing up.

This homeless woman had to be a fraud. She was younger than her mother, made no mention of having other, older daughters, was not strung out on drugs, and her story didn't add up. She never even gave her full name, just calling herself Mrs. Miller, which was a joke, because her mother never married.

Yet, the media jumped on the story. After all, they loved sensationalism. What could be more controversial than a famous actress callously abandoning her own mother? The paparazzi and media were camped out at her gates, awaiting a juicy tidbit to add to their sordid stories. Her agent, assistant, and publicist were deluged with telephone calls, texts, and emails. The headlines were brutal.

"Daphne's Mother Eats Out of Garbage Cans."

"Highest Paid Actress in Hollywood Abandons Mother."

"Daphne's Mother Lives on the Street."

"You Only Have One Mother."

Tears formed in her eyes. Daphne longed for a mother her entire life. She saw how fellow students in school had mothers who dropped them off, and picked them up. They had mothers who bought them clothes, and packed their lunches. They were hugged, and kissed, and loved.

She left for school from a rat-infested apartment building, and a mother high on drugs, in bed with a strange man, and came home to the same scene. Her mother didn't even know she was around. If not for her subsidized lunch, she would have had nothing to eat at home. Her clothes were worn-out, out-of-style hand-me-downs from her older sisters. She couldn't recall ever being hugged or kissed. Only her mother's gritty lovers made such moves. Running away, she knew that she wouldn't be missed.

"Miss Daphne, you have a visitor," her housekeeper announced.

Daphne stopped walking in her solarium, to face the uniformed woman. "Who is it?"

"A River Rutledge."

"River?" For the first time in days, she smiled. River did fly out to be with her. She lied when she told herself that she didn't want to see anyone. River was the one person she really longed to be with.

"He's in the library, ma'am," the housekeeper said, with a smirk.

Daphne raced out of the bright and airy room, and into the

paneled library, with its shelves of books, and leather furniture. River looked like he belonged in the dark and scholarly room. The scent of leather seemed to suit him. He stood in his faded jeans, open collar shirt and tweed blazer. Cowboy boots completed his casual look. His ruffled hair framed his handsome, grinning face. She drew a deep breath, approaching him.

"You came?" she asked, facing him, looking up into his emerald eyes.

"Had to. Friends aren't only for the good times."

He bent to embrace her. Drawing her into his arms, the soft pressure and warmth offered comfort she didn't think she needed. Lowering his face to hers, he kissed her on the lips. Not a kiss of passion, but a gentle kiss of belonging.

"Thank you," she whispered.

"How are you holding up?" He asked.

"I'm managing." She sat on the leather sofa, and patted the spot next to her.

He sat.

He glanced about the room. "Quite a fancy place you have here. It's befitting Hollywood royalty."

"It suits its purpose," she replied, with an answer closer to the truth.

"The media is sure hot on this story."

"Anything controversial and newsworthy. They are always digging for dirt. This time, they aren't going to find any."

"Has there been anything new?"

"We have an investigation taking place."

"You believe she's a fraud?"

She nodded. "My real mother never cared about me. She was so strung out, I'm sure never remembered me. According to Sanjay, she died before I became famous. Her name was Marion Lynn Miller, and she never married."

"The homeless woman calls herself Mrs. Miller."

She stared at him. "You caught that, too?"

"Can't you just get a DNA test, and be done with it?"

"This imposter is not cooperating. She's milking the publicity for all it's worth."

"Sounds like a scheme to get rich off of you."

"And claim her fifteen minutes of fame, at my expense? I'm being raked over the coals."

"When the truth comes out, and it will, you will be the victim." He took her hand in his, and that was reassuring.

With River, she wasn't alone. Throughout her entire life, she was alone. Sure, she had studio people, staff, and acquaintances, but few friends. She had no one to confide in. No one to talk to, or bear her soul. River eased her loneliness. His concern and affection meant more than he could ever realize. She lived a life devoid of the human touch, empathy, and love. He filled the void. His flying out to be with her, eased her mind, and gave her hope. Someone was on her side. Someone who wasn't being paid, but someone who cared.

RIVER WAS glad that he dropped everything and flew out to L.A. to be with Daphne. It was evident that she was hurting and afraid. Having this woman, claiming to be her mother, climbing out of the woodwork, was far more emotional than she let on. He could tell that it conjured up sad memories, better left suppressed. From what she said, her mother threw her away. If she were alive, it was doubtful that she'd ever equate her daughter with Daphne. For a stranger to come forward, as her mother, was like pouring salt on an open wound. He knew that the faster this situation was resolved, the better.

Riverr sat in a wing back chair in front of the fireplace, the warmth of the embers soothing his jet lag. The suite was spacious, more like a small apartment, than a guest room. It was cozy, and not sterile, like hotel suites. Daphne's practicality was evident, as it had all of the amenities. There was a bar, coffee-tea service, a mini refrigerator stocked with beverages and snacks, a flat screen monitor for television or computer. The king-sized bed had a down comforter, and pillows galore. French doors led to a balcony, with a view of the L.A. skyline. Like a hotel, the bathroom had everything a guest would require, even a plush bathrobe, which he was wearing.

Sipping an aperitif cognac, his mind replayed the day. The flight, on his Lear jet, was uneventful. Being picked up at the airport by a stretch limousine was a pleasant welcome. Entering the gates to her estate, through a swarm of paparazzi and reporters, was jarring. Rolling up the cobbled stone drive, he realized that one could spend a lifetime at her compound, never having to leave. Her palatial home, though expected, was over-the-top. The interior was even more grand than the exterior. Traditional, everything was the opposite of his contemporary, minimalist lifestyle. Opposites attract.

When Daphne entered the library, she reminded him of a shattered little girl. Her lips trembled when she spoke. Her bloodshot eyes revealed many tears. She looked small and vulnerable. He had to hug her, and even her body quivered. She needed someone. He was that someone.

He had always taken his family for granted. As an only child, he was doted upon, and never lacking in material things or love. His parents had a loving, long-term marriage. They lived as equals. He was encouraged from a young age to pursue his dreams. Using their resources, they made it happen. College, world travel, graduate school, they were there for him. Even now, they listened to him, offered advice, and encouraged him. When he visited them, he felt energized, and loved. He swore that when he married, if he married, he would raise his children to be as confident, and as loved as he.

Listening to Daphne made him sad. When she talked about her past while they were in Italy, he found it shocking. This intelligent and beautiful woman had to fend for herself from a young age. She didn't have a support system, resources or love. Yet, somehow, she found fame and fortune. Listening to her tonight, he wondered what price she had to pay. She had all the material goods that money could buy, but she didn't have a family. She was basically an orphan, alone in the world.

To have a stranger enter her life, and turn it upside down was unfair. At dinner, she talked about the importance of her career, and her reputation. If she had a mother who actually raised her, and supported her, she would never be out living on the streets or eating from garbage cans. Through the years, she had guilt over her mother and siblings, even though they ignored her. To them she never existed. How many times, she was going to try to find them, but realized what a futile effort it would be. Her mother tried to pass her on to dirty old pedophiles as their next plaything. Her sisters would be begging for drug money. Better to let it go, and move on. She rose above it all. Her biggest fear was having it all crumble. She didn't want to end up where it all began.

River had heard of the "homeless bag lady syndrome." It was something that many successful women suffered from. It was the fear that one day they would lose everything they worked for, and, in later years, they would be thrust to live on the streets.

He assured Daphne that he was there for her. She had no worries. They were going to get through this blip in life, together. This episode would be resolved, and forgotten.

As he stared into the flames, he pondered his future, their future. How foolish of him, wanting to write Daphne off, because she was a jet-setting actress. She was right. Daphne was her persona. Inside, she was kind and vulnerable Meg. She was a real person, and a decent human being. Tonight, Meg came out, the Meg he fell in love with. She was the only woman he fell in love with. Her appeal was more than sexual chemistry. He loved her personality, her mind, and, even her ambition. Knowing how she worked her way to the top, in one of the most impossible professions, he was in awe of her. She didn't sell her body, or her soul for success. She did it the hard way, through her talent.

There was something about her. She just clicked with him. Tonight, as they sipped coffee, after dinner, he realized that he could spend a lifetime with her, and never get bored.

He kissed her good night, and he saw his future in her eyes. He could wipe away the tears of her past.

21

"Mrs. Miller has been cornered," Les Porter, Daphne's agent proclaimed, when he came to her home the next day.

He had telephoned in the morning to say that he had an update on the controversy. Daphne invited him to join she and River for lunch. They were seated in the sun room, surrounded by walls of glass, tropical greenery, and the bubbling water from a marble fountain. The Victorian wicker table was set with vintage china, crystal and sterling. Daphne held court, while her staff served salad, rolls, and French onion soup, to start.

"Les, I like what I'm hearing," Daphne said, staring at him with eager anticipation.

Les fanned his napkin on his lap. "The investigation has found that this Mrs. Miller is neither homeless, nor your mother."

"Surprise of surprises."

"She's a fraud. Her name is Eleanor Smith, and she's from Iowa, a retired factory worker."

"Why would she target me? How would she know about my past?" Daphne asked, a chill coursing through her body.

"When visiting Chicago, she met one of Sanjay's staff in a hotel bar. He told her about the project. She took it from there," Les explained, taking a sip of water from his goblet.

"Sanjay will be livid," River interrupted.

"For sure," Daphne said.

"Eleanor used to do community theater, and aspired to be an actress, when she was younger," Les added. "You'd think she was gunning for an Oscar, with the performances she's given to the press."

"Now, what?" Daphne asked.

"Your attorney is speaking with her attorney."

"I hope this isn't involving money. She's a fraud, and shouldn't get a dime." Daphne let out a sigh, eyes blazing.

"It involves her coming clean, or going to jail," Les raked a finger through his silver hair.

"People will still think that I paid her off, to make her go away. It won't restore my reputation."

"Daphne, she will be asked to take a DNA test. Sanjay's documentary will also set the record straight."

"Why would she do this to me?"

"Money, and a last crack at fame."

"Well, she got her fifteen minutes of fame."

"There are a lot of opportunistic, crazy people out there. It's amazing that this hasn't happened earlier."

"I worked hard to get where I am, only to have people think that I owe them, or that they own me. It's so wrong," Daphne felt the tears pooling in her eyes. She swiped at them.

River took her hand under the table. His reassuring touch made her heart stop racing, and she drew a deep breath of calm.

"So much is wrong in this world," Les said. "You are still too young to realize it, yet." He took a roll from a bread basket, and ripped it in half, before placing it on his bread plate. River cleared his throat. "Well, it looks like the problem is solved, or soon will be. I propose a toast."

River lifted his Mimosa-filled glass. Daphne and Les did the same.

"A toast to the blips in life, and to a bright and cheery future."

"Here, here," Les added.

They clinked glasses.

RIVER KNEW that Daphne was scheduled to appear at a news conference, with her attorney. She dressed in a demure, yet stylish houndstooth suit. The ruffled hem line and Laboutin pumps added Hollywood flair. Her long, dark hair was up in a French twist, and her makeup was flawless. River watched on his office computer. After his short weekend visit to L.A., he returned home to a mountain of work. A new product was being released, and he had to work with his public relations and marketing teams to make it a success. His situation was far different than Daphne's. He was promoting a product, while she was protecting her reputation.

He could tell that she was nervous, from the way she swayed on her high heels, and fingered her hair. The paparazzi and media surrounded her, as she and her attorney stood behind a wood podium and microphone. Her attorney, a distinguished white-haired man, made an opening statement. River thought that he sounded like he was in a courtroom, defending Daphne as the victim of a scam.

"Miss Miller is the innocent party in an elaborate scheme to swindle funds from her, by a cold and heartless opportunist. Imagine, someone claiming to be your wronged mother, when your real mother has been deceased for years. Yet, your reputation is tarnished by the false allegations. You, the press, have run with this story, promoting it as truth, without researching it, or giving Daphne the benefit of a doubt. Shame on you," he began.

The press was uncharacteristically, eerily quiet.

He continued, "Daphne's real mother is Marion Lynn Miller, buried in a pauper's cemetery outside of Chicago. She died before Daphne became famous, and never married. The fraudulent 'Mrs. Miller' is really Eleanor Smith, a retired factory worker and actress, from Iowa. While visiting Chicago, she learned of an upcoming documentary on Daphne, and saw an opportunity. She and her counsel denied the allegations. A court order required her to provide a DNA sample for testing. The test concluded that Ms. Smith, and Daphne are not related. We ask that you retract your stories, that have damaged Miss Miller, and offer an apology. Daphne ..."

The attorney stepped aside, and Daphne approached the podium. River could see the tears swelling in her eyes, as she fought to contain them. He swallowed hard. He wished that he could have been there to offer some emotional support and comfort. The photographers were all over themselves.

"Thank you." She nodded to her attorney. "It is said that it takes a lifetime to create a good reputation, and a moment to ruin it. I have struggled, and worked hard to attain success. Most people don't know my story, my rise from poverty and the streets, to the fortune and glamour of Hollywood. I was hoping to tell my life story, in a soon-to-be-released documentary, about my 'Like Home' foundation. It's sad that a stranger would use my life as a method of extorting money, and getting publicity. If I had been blessed with a loving and supportive mother, I would have done everything I could to assure her a comfortable life. She wouldn't have been abandoned on the streets. It's sad that so many believed this sordid lie. Instead of coming to me, this situation was spread by the press. I find this unfortunate and sad. To believe a stranger, without any research or background check, is unconscionable. I am owed a retraction, and an apology. As for Ms. Smith, I hope that she receives the mental health treatment she so desperately needs."

Daphne moved away from the podium. Her attorney took her place. The press yelled out a jumble of questions, jockeying for positions closer to the podium. Cameras blinked.

"We will not be taking questions," her attorney stated. "Our statements spoke for themselves."

He took Daphne by the arm, and led her toward a waiting limousine. She disappeared within the stretch car.

River clicked off the news. Daphne was very poised and eloquent, speaking without notes. He could only wonder what was going through her mind.

THAT EVENING, Daphne sat in her bed, sipping tea. The house was quiet, save for the ticking of mantle clock above the fireplace in her bedroom suite. She liked to gaze at the gilded antique clock, that she had procured in Paris years earlier. It had been one of her first purchases when she received the proceeds of her first film. She snuggled under a down comforter, wearing a flannel granny gown. So much for being a sex symbol. No, she didn't sleep in the nude.

Her mind wandered to the news conference, and, after, when she was whisked home. Her attorney dropped her off, and he returned to his office. Angie descended on her with telephone messages and e-mails. She waved her away. Instead, she went up to her bedroom to escape. Donning her flannel nightgown, she went to bed for a nap. Awakening in time for dinner, she supped alone in her room. After the dishes were removed, she sat with her tea.

She required closure from recent events. Having to mentally relive her childhood, and defend herself from lies and accusations gave her headaches and heart palpitations. She was trembling at the podium. Her acting prowess saved her. She was able to appear calm and together. Inside, she was falling apart.

Through the years, she missed having a family. Co-stars had parents and siblings, grandparents, aunts and uncles, and cousins. Some had spouses and children, even grandchildren. Even her staff had family. They attended family celebrations, milestones, and holidays. She was always alone.

Her entire life was lived as a solitary being. She supported herself, and lived by herself. To the outside world, she was an independent woman, who lived life on her own terms. Not being accountable to anyone, she was an empowered and liberated woman. Inside, she was lonely. There was heartache, when you had no one to share the intimacies of your life. Holidays were superficial, when you didn't have family to share memories, and make memories. She didn't have scrapbooks or photo albums documenting her childhood. No memories. No baby book, or mementoes. No heirlooms. No family photographs on the mantle. Tears seeped from her eyes.

Maybe it was a trade-off. She was bestowed bankable good looks, talent, fame and fortune. In turn, she would be denied a life of normalcy, of affection, and love.

When her private cellphone rang, she was tempted to ignore it. When she glanced at the caller ID, she saw that it was River. She drew a deep breath, wondering if she really wanted to speak to him. She hadn't spoken to anyone since she came home, requesting quiet and solitude.

She picked up the phone, and said hello.

"Hey, Meg, for a moment there, I thought that you weren't answering, and weren't home," Rivers cheerful voice came through.

"I've been home. Actually, I've been in my room since I returned from the news conference."

"Are you okay? You sound rather sad."

"I'll be okay." She sighed. "Just feeling sorry for myself."

"I'd think that you'd be elated. Having that fake woman out of your life, and the truth made public is a cause for celebration."

"You'd think. It's just made me reflect about my past, and ponder my future."

The past is over and done. Your future is bright."

He sounded so upbeat and positive.

"If I were there, I'd have you get dressed, and we would be out on the town: a candlelight dinner, jazz club, a moonlight walk, a nightcap by your pool. Maybe a little skinny dipping." He chuckled.

She had to smile.

"I'd love to see you skinny dipping." She laughed.

"I'd love to get you naked."

She squirmed under the covers.

"Are you in bed?" he asked.

"As a matter of fact, yes."

"Damn, if I were closer, I'd be right over to join you."

His words were making her warm and fuzzy. Her funk was lifting.

"You know, things are going to be looking up from now on," he said.

"You think?"

"Sanjay says that the documentary is going to broaden your appeal, and popularity. It showcases a part of you, people don't know, but will relate to. That little incident with the fake mom was actually great publicity."

"You know, for someone who has been disinterested in my career, and detests publicity, this isn't making sense."

"I'll admit, I want to cheer you up. I also need to change the subject, or I will be dialing up my pilot to fly out tonight, just to get in your bed."

"Better than my sofa?" Her mind wandered to the little apartment above The Classy Chassis.

"Much better. Anyway, I'm sure that we will be getting together soon," he said.

"I'm sure that Sanjay told you that the documentary is in the editing stage. It's going to premiere at Sundance, and may end up at Cannes. A trip to the French Riviera could be scheduled for May."

"You know what I think of premieres."

"You can skip Sundance, but, if you want to get me in bed, Cannes is a pretty romantic location."

22

For Daphne, Cannes brought back memories of Salerno. The French Riviera was much like the Amalfi coast. Both featured hilly, seaside villas and structures, scenic historical town centers, cathedrals and castles, sandy beaches, and Mediterranean ports. Cannes was, however, more of a high-end beach resort for the rich and famous. Once a year, for twelve days in May, the international film community descended on the quiet town, for the renowned film festival. As a famous actress, Daphne had attended the event during the past ten years. Spending a few days at the luxurious International Carlton hotel, promoting her films and career, and winning awards had been marked on her yearly calendar. This year was different, in so many ways. She was attending as the subject of a documentary. Before, her appearance was due to an acclaimed role in a motion picture. Flying overseas with River was also a new experience. Cannes was something she attended by herself, save for her entourage of staff. Bringing a date was special. Sharing her suite with someone was new. Contrary to what the public thought, she spent her nights alone, usually with a book for company.

River was reluctant to join her. She knew of his disdain for Hollywood schmoozing. She assured him that he wouldn't have any official duties, other than join her at a couple of social events. He would be spared the press conferences, photo-ops, and Red Carpet. He was more of a loner, and his tech business allowed it. Hers was a very public profession. In order to make the relationship work, she knew that she had to abide by his wishes, and he, hers.

He joined she and her staff in her sleek Gulfstream. The plane was fitted with all the amenities to make an overseas trip comfortable. She had her pilot fly from L.A. to Midway, to pick up River. From there, the ten-hour flight to France was smooth, and uneventful. Landing at Nice Cote d'Azur airport, a limousine drove the thirty minutes to Cannes.

The International Carlton was an imposing white monolithic structure with turrets, located on the Mediterranean. Rows of towering palm trees lined the walk and stairway to the hotel's pillared main entrance. A clock and fluttering international flags were above the portico. As they pulled up to the hotel, the ever-present paparazzi descended like vultures after prey. Daphne drew a deep breath for courage, as she always had. The harassment was a part of being famous.

"Sparkle," Daphne whispered.

River smiled, and muttered, "Sparkle."

The chauffeur opened the door, and Daphne slid out of the seat in her vivacious and confident way. She had dressed for the camera, before landing. The floral, cotton halter dress enhanced her slim, well-endowed figure. The skirt billowed in the mild sea breeze, revealing a hint of leg, as she stood inhaling the salty air. Smiling, she waved for the cameras, and the fans who were gathering around the hotel steps.

River eased out of the limousine, and followed her a couple of feet behind, trying to avoid the spotlight. Daphne knew how uncomfortable crowds made him. He was shifting on his feet.

While she chatted with the press, she glanced at him, as he walked up the hotel steps, to wait for her in the contemporary, open lobby, as planned.

When she entered the lobby, she took his hand, and they passed the white pillars, pedestals with vases of fresh flowers, the grand staircase with its iron rails, and under the metal chandeliers, and scurried to the elevators. Once in the cab, she sighed.

"We made it. A little solitude before the cocktail party," she said.

"What cocktail party?"

"I'm hosting a small cocktail party in a conference room for everyone affiliated with the documentary," Daphne explained.

"I think Sanjay said something about it."

"Yes, he's attending. He's picking up Kemsit at the airport, first."

"Interesting." River rubbed his chin.

"She agreed to be his date for the festival. Since she usually takes an annual trip to Egypt, she thought she'd tag it to Cannes. After all, it's only a four-hour or so flight to Cairo from here."

"Okay. I still find it interesting."

"Sanjay and Kemsit are friends. This is a big deal for him."

"And for you."

"Glad you came?" She met his gaze.

"I don't know, yet. I do want to support Sanjay, and you." He squeezed her hand.

THEY EXITED the elevator on the seventh floor.

"This is the luxury floor. I reserved my favorite corner suite. It has wrap-around balconies, with the most amazing views of the sea and the town." Daphne led him down the hall, their footsteps silenced by the carpet.

"Lovely hotel."

"It was featured in the Cary Grant, Grace Kelly film, 'To Catch a Thief.'"

"Better watch your diamonds." He chuckled.

"Actually, I never bring good jewelry here. This hotel has been the scene of several high-profile jewel heists."

"Gee, I learn something new every day. Why do you stay here?"

She shrugged. "I love old Hollywood lore."

At the door at the end of the hall, they stopped. Daphne took the key card from her pocket, and inserted it in the lock. Clicking the door open, she entered. River followed. Daphne drew a deep breath. The scent of fresh cut flowers, arranged in a vase, set on an end table, wafted in the breeze from the open French doors leading to the balcony. She liked the familiarity of places when she traveled. When she found accommodations she liked, she booked them regularly. This was her home-away-from-home in Cannes.

"Nice place," River commented, walking into the suite, hands in his pocket, looking around, as he peered in each room.

Daphne liked the simplicity of the suite. The muted tan, gold, and cream colors of the walls, draperies, and furnishings were calming. Oriental rugs added a splash of color. The living room was perfect for intimate conversation. The dining room had an oval table with curved chairs. The table was set for two, with white linen, fine china, crystal and silver. Red roses in an ornate gilded vase were the centerpiece. A kitchenette featured blonde cabinetry and white counters. There was every amenity a person desired.

After coming from inspecting the bathroom, River said, "Two pedestal sinks, a whirlpool tub, large shower, and a sofa. A bathroom with many romantic possibilities."

He winked, and she rubbed her arms from the tingling.

"There are two bedrooms and baths," he added.

"One must always have space for guests."

"Am I a guest?" He cocked and eyebrow.

"That depends."

"On?"

She laughed, walking to the open doors, and stepping out on to the balcony. River followed. Late morning brought sunshine and mellow breezes. Yachts were gliding into the harbor below. More guests for the film festival, she surmised. Some people sailed in on their private vessels. She looked out at the hotel's pier, jutting out into the turquoise Mediterranean. The beach below was filled with cabanas and chaises. Palm trees stood like sentinels, everywhere. A church bell chimed.

"Lovely, isn't it?" She looked up at River, who stood next to her, peering out at the view.

"Very. It is similar to Salerno."

"That's why I figured you'd like it. During the festival, though, this town will be wall-to-wall people, I'm afraid. Yet, it adds to the festive atmosphere."

"Well, I've heard of Cannes, but never experienced it," he said.

"Here's your lucky chance."

He draped an arm around her shoulders. "Why a hotel, and not a villa?"

"It depends on the location, and the purpose. This hotel is huge, but offers solitude. Cannes can be busy and stressful. I prefer to have a place to myself, that is intimate, quiet, and private. My staff and crew can't just pop in. They know that they have to call first. Sharing a villa, is like having a bunch of roommates."

"Thank you for allowing me to be a guest-roommate." He squeezed her shoulder. He had to know that he meant more than that.

"Thank you for joining me."

He drew her into his arms, and her heart quickened. She grew warm, as he pulled her in to him. Lowering his head, he met her lips and kissed her. She returned the kiss, circling her arms around his neck. Deeper kisses had her lightheaded, and she groaned. His gaze met hers with such depth that her eyes teared.

"This is the Meg I love," he whispered, and kissed her on the cheek. Releasing her, he stepped aside.

She continued to look at him, his silhouette against the backdrop of the scenic view, as if he belonged there. He did belong ... with her. He said that he loved her. Someone loved her. She dreamed of being loved, her entire life. Love seemed elusive. Would someone ever love her? What was love? How would she know if, or when she found it? Looking at River, she realized that he was love. No one touched her, and understood her like he did. He loved the "real" Meg, not the superficial Daphne.

"Hungry? I'll have the concierge order, and send up a butler with lunch." She pointed toward the dining room.

He cleared his throat. "That's probably a good idea."

"We can decide what our plans are before the party. If we have plans, or we can just recover from jet lag here," she said, her mind reeling with lurid thoughts about the two of them enjoying the suite, and each other.

AFTER LUNCH, River had Meg for dessert. He snickered, as he stood, drink in hand, at the cocktail party at the Carlton Bar. Meg, rather Daphne, was making the rounds with guests. He liked to watch her mingle. Even with dark hair, she played the part of a bombshell. Her signature walk, and soft voice set her apart in the crowded space. Wearing a skin tight red bandage dress also helped. To think that he had spent the early afternoon playing in bed with her. Making love to her was easy.

Though she was physically desirable, her mind was as stimulating. He liked that, a lot.

He caught Sanjay and Kemsit heading his way across the shiny floor. Sanjay was dapper in a navy pinstripe suit and geometric tie. His turban matched the tie, perfectly. Kemsit held his arm. She was poured into a sparkly gold mini dress with fringe. They looked exotic, and good together. Their darker complexion and stunning looks made them look very Hollywood.

"The man of the hour," River greeted.

The men shook hands.

"How does it feel being a star?" River teased.

Sanjay chuckled. "It feels good, actually. I dreamed of being at Cannes, and want to pinch myself. Thanks to Daphne, here I am."

"Thanks to your talent. You've been working toward this goal for years," River said.

Sanjay clicked his cocktail glass against River's. "Cheers."

"Cheers," Kemsit added, clicking her glass to theirs.

"It's wonderful that you came, Kemsit. Daphne has been looking forward to seeing you," River said.

"We're meeting for brunch tomorrow," Kemsit said.

"Sanjay said that you are off to Egypt, when you leave here?"

She nodded. "I try to get to Cairo at least once a year. When I was invited here, I thought I'd add Egypt, since it's so close."

"Do you have family there?" River asked.

Kemsit shifted on her heels. "It's complicated."

River watched Daphne breeze over to join them. Her poise and elegance exuded the aura of a star.

"Having fun?" she asked.

"Lots," Kemsit said, with a broad smile.

"When this party ends, I have reservations for four for dinner on the Carlton pier. We are going to dine in style, with

a fabulous view. The company will be even better." She
winked.

DAPHNE HAD NEVER HAD SO much fun in Cannes. During her
previous visits, her social life consisted of obligatory parties
and events. Her days were scheduled. As an actress in a nomi-
nated film, her schedule was booked by the studio's publicity
department and her staff. Cannes, like most film festivals and
premieres, were all business. There was little down time.
Always alone, she was more like a caricature of herself. She was
on display.

This year was different. She was attending as the subject of
a documentary, not a typical leading lady carrying a film.
Sanjay was as much a friend as a producer. With he, River and
Kemsit present, she had friends. If the film festival were a cake,
River was the frosting. Instead of being alone in her suite, she
had River to share it with. For the first time, she had a man in
her bed, and she liked it. She liked it a lot. River was loving,
caring, gentle, with just enough fire to make things interesting.

The day after the cocktail party, she enjoyed brunch with
Kemsit, a true friend. After, she joined River for a tour of
Cannes. It was impossible to be incognito in such a busy place,
where almost everyone there was famous. The paparazzi had
far too many celebrities to cover, to be at more than one place
at a time.

They strolled *La Croisette,* the mile-long promenade, lined
with luxury hotels, boutiques, and casinos on the shore side,
and sandy beaches and glamorous yachts docked on the sea
side. Outside of the tourist office, stars were planted on the
sidewalk, like Hollywood's Grauman's Chinese Theatre.
Daphne pointed out her star. They walked the high-end shopping street, *Rue d'Antibes.* After, they strolled the quays at Vieux

Port. At *Quai Sainte-Pierre*, they perused the luxury yachts, leisure boats, and fishing boats. As they watched the sun set, a magical golden glow enveloped the port side buildings.

"Incredible," River muttered.

"Magical," Daphne added.

"You are magical," River said, leaning in to kiss her on the lips.

"I bet that will make the morning news," she whispered.

"At his point, I don't care. Do you?"

"No. Not at all."

"Maybe it's time that the whole world knows that I am in love with you, and that I want to spend the rest of my life with you," River said.

She peered up into his glittering emerald eyes, and her heart melted. Tears formed. For so long, she wondered if she would ever be loved. River was in love with her.

"I'm in love with you," she admitted. For the first time in her life, she was loved and in love. There was comfort and security with River. They were equals, and understood the stress of career success, and had the resources to make a long-distance life work. She saw the future in his eyes.

THE TIME in Cannes was a turning point in their relationship. Viewing the documentary to rounds of applause, an exquisite, romantic, three-course, Mediterranean dinner at *L'Assiette Provencale*, and a visit to *Le Croisette Barireiere de Cannes*, the casino, and making love in the quiet of the suite, rounded out an evening. An early morning stroll to *Marche-Forville,* the famous indoor market, for breakfast baguettes began the big day.

That evening, while River stood at the top of the stairs at the famous home of the Cannes International Film Festival, the *Palais des Festivals des Congres*, Daphne emerged from her limousine. The billboard above the entrance announced the festival, while the famous red carpet graced the walk, stairs and landing. This was the prestigious awards night, the highlight of the event.

Daphne whispered, "Sparkle," before slipping out of the limousine, on to the carpet, and under the canopy. River preferred for her to be alone in the spotlight. Knowing that he was up at the entrance waiting for her, made her smile, a real smile. She had selected a statement gown for the occasion. The form-fitting strapless sapphire blue silk gown, with translucent overlay of beads and sparkling crystals, fit the bill. As she walked, a long, translucent train trailed behind. At the landing, midway up the wide stairway, she paused, turned, posing for the photographers. This was traditional. The applause was deafening. She flipped her long, dark hair over her shoulder, and continued to walk up the stairs. Seeing River waiting for her, she wondered if this is what her wedding would be like.

At the entrance, she took his hand, and entered the cavernous lobby. Sanjay was already there with Kemsit on his arm. He was beaming, as this was his big night, too. They were led into the Lumiere Theatre, the grand auditorium with red draperies framing the stage, and matching red upholstery of the numerous seats. They sat in the front row.

Daphne drew a deep breath, as she always had at award events. Her competitive nature came out. River squeezed her hand, and her nerves calmed. She glanced back at the crowded theater. Even the mezzanine was packed. The chattering of voices reverberated into a loud roar. Only when the lights dimmed, and the massive screen on stage lit with graphics, did the space grow silent.

She listened to the speeches, watched the film clips, and applauded as awards were presented. When the award for best documentary, the *LCEil dor*, was next, she sat tall, and drew a deep breath. When her documentary was listed as a finalist, her heart beat so fast, she thought she might faint. She had to look around, when it was announced as the award winner. Only when Sanjay approached to take her hand, did she truly believe that it won. The applause was deafening, as he led her up on the stage. She stood, frozen. This was not an ordinary award. This was honoring her life journey. As she peered out into the audience, her eyes misted. The audience stood and applauded. She swallowed hard. The documentary bared her secrets, and her soul. In silence, she thanked the scared little girl, who survived life in the projects, a mother and siblings with addictions, who ran away, and created a fairy tale life. She thought of how she tried to give back, through her foundation, so that other frightened children wouldn't struggle as she had. Gazing out into the front row, she saw River, beaming, as he clapped. She had come so far.

Sanjay began to speak, and she listened. He explained the origins of the project, and thanked her for the opportunity to document her life, and her foundation. After, the spotlight shone on her.

Daphne drew a deep breath, and began to speak, "Thank you for the honor of this award. Out of all of the awards I have won, this one is the most meaningful and special. When I was a little girl, I dreamed of being an actress, as many children do. Hollywood seemed so far away, and unattainable. After all, how could a child born in to illegitimacy, addiction, and poverty ever amount to anything? I took a chance, and ran away. I struggled, lied about my age, waitressed, scrimped and saved. I took acting lessons, and performed in any theater where I won an audition for a part. I was lucky. I was discovered by Les Porter, the best agent an actress could hope for. I avoided casting couches and deceit. My career blossomed and thrived. Choice roles won me acclaim, awards, and made me independently wealthy. Yet, I am still that scared little girl, inside. I want to make a difference in the lives of other scared little girls, and boys. There is hope. You are worthy of a better life. You have a successful future, in whatever profession you wish to pursue. Where you come from doesn't matter. It's where you go. This award is for you."

She dabbed her eyes, and took a breath, continuing, "I want to thank the judges at the Cannes Film Festival for recognizing this special documentary on my foundation, 'Like Home.' Sanjay, there would be no film without your amazing research and talent. I learned a great deal about myself through your lens. I want to thank the town of Cairo, Illinois, for welcoming me as one of your own. Kemsit, you are a true friend. Most of all, I want to thank River Rutledge for loving me, with all of my faults, my crazy life, and personalities. I love you."

ACKNOWLEDGMENTS

I have dedicated this book to Middle Eastern belly dance performers, because they have exemplified the culture, history, beauty, elegance and drama of this exotic art form.

To dance on a stage, in a restaurant, club, a home, business, dance workshop, hafla, festival is an accomplishment. As a performer, a dancer is an educator, as well as an entertainer. The music, costuming, makeup, props and choreography reveal the different influences and aspects of this mysterious dance.

As someone who is a family-friendly professional belly dance performer, I know how it feels to be put on display. I've graced stages, danced regularly with a live band, performed singing telegrams, and entertained at private parties and events. Each situation is unique, and calls for a different skill. More than dance, a performance is part personality and part public relations. As a performer, you are representing the dance to the general public. You are the dance.

I also enjoy watching other dancers. Each dancer adds her own nuance to this ancient art form. Belly dance lends itself to individuality. No two dancers are, or should be, alike. Observing other dancers is also an education.

To the public, there is far more to belly dance than "shaking the booty." Belly dancers are trained professionals, with a demanding skill set. Before performing, dancers have studied for years, and practiced for hours, just as in other forms of dance. If something looks easy, it's not. A true professional just makes it look easy.

Belly dance is sensual, not sexual. It is mysterious and ancient. If you haven't attended a live belly dance performance, please plan on it. You will be glad that you did.

ABOUT THE AUTHOR

Nancy Loyan (aka: Nailah) has studied and performed the art of Middle Eastern belly dance for over 30 years, with national and international instructors. In the Summer of 2008, she traveled to Egypt to attend the *Ahlan Wa Sahlan* dance festival in Cairo, where she studied with Egypt's greatest dancers: Dina, Randa Kamel, Mona El Saeid, Dr. Mo Geddawi and Regaey, and had the pleasure of dancing a solo on a Nile River cruise ship.

She taught dance at studios, recreation centers, and regularly at the Chautauqua Institution in Chautauqua, New York, where she was once featured in their advertising campaign. She has danced before their prestigious Dance Circle, the first non-ballet person to do so, and has been featured in the *Chautauquan Daily* newspaper and on Jamestown radio. She has presented workshops and dance seminars at women's wellness retreats around the country, and has taught at Lakeside, Ohio.

A world traveler, Nailah has toured France, Italy, Greece, Great Britain, South America, the Seychelles Islands, the Caribbean, all over the United States including Hawaii, Canada, and Egypt.

In her "other" life, she is Nancy Loyan, a multi-published writer and women's fiction-romance author. As a freelance writer, she specialized in architecture and construction, antique safes, belly dance and special interest. She has instructed writing for the Cuyahoga County Public Library system, Shaker Arts Council and the Chautauqua Institution. Her novel, *A Kiss in the Rain* was featured in The Chautauqua Bookstore, where she had a very successful book signing in the Author's Alcove in 2015. She has published over a dozen novels in multiple genres, that "unlock the barriers to love." Her latest project is this book series based on Middle Eastern dance.

www.nancyloyan.com
www.NailahDance.com

www.ingramcontent.com/pod-product-compliance
Lightning Source LLC
Chambersburg PA
CBHW071240130626
46556CB00003B/1089